YOU CAN TEACH YOURSELF® AUTOHARP

By Meg Peterson

CD Contents*

1. Introduction & Explanation (1:34)
2. Simple Back-Up Strums (2:52)
3. L'il Liza Jane/Page 23 (1:39)
4. Red River Valley/Page 25 (1:55)
5. Amazing Grace/Page 28 (2:08)
6. Cindy/Page 31 (2:49)
7. Introducing the Index Finger/Page 32 (1:55)
8. The Argpeggiando Stroke/Page 34 (1:25)
9. Streets of Laredo/Page 35 (2:56)
10. The Church Lick/Page 39 (2:09)
11. When the Saints Go Marching In/Page 40 (1:09)
12. Camptown Races/Page 43 & 69 (1:38)
13. Scratch Style/Page 44 (2:13)
14. Sweet Betsy from Pike/Page 46 (1:19)
15. The Crawdad Song/Page 51 (2:03)
16. Scarborough Fair/Page 55 (:48)
17. Swing Low, Sweet Chariot/Page 56 (1:20)
18. Travis Picking/Page 57 (1:29)
19. The More We Get Together/Page 58 (1:19)
20. Michael, Row Your Boat/Page 59 (2:06)
21. Learning to Play Melody/Page 62 (4:29)
22. Row, Row, Row Your Boat/Page 65 (:49)
23. Jacob's Ladder/Page 67 (2:07)
24. Battle Hymn/Page 70 (1:29)
25. Filler Strokes/Page 71 (2:34)
26. Down in the Valley/Page 73 &14 (:50)
27. Wildwood Flower/Page 74 (:40)
28. Calypso Strumming/Page 78 (1:37)
29. The Sloop "John B"/Page 79 (1:28)
30. Blues & Jazz/Page 81 & 82 (3:01)
31. Rock-A-My Soul//Page 91 (1:46)

*This book is available as a book only or as a book/compact disc configuration.

If you have purchased the book only, a recording (95024CD) of the music in this book is now available. The publisher strongly recommends the use of this resource along with the text to insure accuracy of interpretation and ease in learning.

© 1994 BY MEL BAY PUBLICATIONS, INC., PACIFIC, MO 63069.
ALL RIGHTS RESERVED. INTERNATIONAL COPYRIGHT SECURED. B.M.I. MADE AND PRINTED IN U.S.A.
No part of this publication may be reproduced in whole or in part, or stored in a retrieval system, or transmitted in any form or by any means, electronic, mechanical, photocopy, recording, or otherwise, without written permission of the publisher.

Visit us on the Web at www.melbay.com — E-mail us at email@melbay.com

1 2 3 4 5 6 7 8 9 0

PREFACE

The Autoharp is one of the most rewarding and adaptable of musical instuments. It can be played simply, by stroking one chord at a time to accompany singing; as a solo melody instrument; or as a rhythm back-up in a group, incorporating a variety of complicated picking styles. It has been hailed as a uniquely American musical instument because, even though originally invented in Germany in 1884 by Karl August Gutter, * it was widely popularized in the United States by another inventor and modifier of harps, Charles Zimmerman. He manufactured Gutter's chorded zither in order to promote a new kind of musical scoring system. Zimmerman's system never caught on, but his tool for demonstrating it, which he renamed the Autoharp, flourished. At the turn of the century, it was all the rage. John Philip Sousa had dozens of Autoharps in his band, and W.C. Handy, the father of the blues, called it his "good luck piece." By 1929, however, the Autoharp's popularity had declined drastically, and fewer than 600 instruments were made. But it was the unique sound of this instrument, appealing to the musicians of the Appalachians—Ernest V. "Pop" Stoneman, Kilby Snow, and especially the Carter family—that probably saved the Autoharp from extinction.

Over the past thirty years the Autoharp has enjoyed an astounding revival, becoming a very popular solo instrument, not only as an integral part of string bands and bluegrass combos, which have their roots in the music of the Appalachian mountains, but at the Grand Old Opry, and in concert halls and folk festivals around the world. This very versatile instrument can be played in an endless variety of styles, from country to popular to classical. It has taken its place as a teaching tool in elementary classrooms, colleges, and music schools. Churches, missions in the Third World, rehabilitation hospitals, camps, private homes, and senior citizen centers use and cherish their Autoharps. Everybody loves to play music—it provides an important intangible, powerful dimension to our lives—and here is an instrument that gives the gift of musical participation to everybody!

How you play the Autoharp depends on your determinaion, ingenuity, and imagination. You can go as far as you want. But first, I urge you to become acquainted with the instrument. Learn to tune it, to change the strings, and to care for it. Start at the beginning of this book and work your way to the end. Each song teaches something new and each strum pattern is built on the previous one. When you have practiced each selection and perfected each strum, you will have the necessary foundation to go on to more advanced styles and more intricate picking.

The songs in this book are arranged for the 15 chord instrument, since it is the most popular for beginning students. For more advanced players with 21 to 27 chord instruments, who may wish to use this book as a teaching text, detailed lessons on harmony and transposition (changing a song from one key to the other) are presented in **The Complete Method for Autoharp or Chromaharp* and *Let's Play the Autoharp*.

Enjoy this book. Share it with your friends. Exchange ideas about new licks and new songs. But most of all, enjoy making music!

Meg Peterson
Maplewood, N.J.
August, 1994

*For more information on the history of the Autoharp see p. 3-6, *Autoharp Quarterly*, Vol. 3, April, 1991, P.O. Box A, Newport, PA 17074.

**For study of advanced strumming techniques: *The Complete Method For Autoharp Or Chromaharp* by Meg Peterson, Mel Bay Publications, 1979, and *Mel Bay's Complete Book of Traditional & Country Autoharp Picking Styles* by Meg Peterson, Mel Bay Publications, 1986. For more study of transposition and harmony: *Let's Play The Autoharp* by Meg Peterson, Mel Bay Publications, 1981.

TABLE OF CONTENTS

	Page
CARE OF THE AUTOHARP; Tuning, Changing strings	5
HOW TO HOLD THE AUTOHARP; Choosing a pick, How to stroke; Playing a one chord song	8
CHANGING CHORDS; Two chord songs; Basic time signatures	12
FINGERING; Three chord songs; A word about transposition	15
SIMPLE BACK-UP STRUMS; in 4/4; in 3/4; in 6/8	22
COMBINING UP AND DOWN STROKES; Introducing the index finger	30
THE ARPEGGIANDO STROKE; Holding the Autoharp Appalachian style	34
THE CHURCH LICK; Playing with the loose fist	39
APPALACHIAN STRUMS:	42
BASIC THUMB LICK; 2/4 time	42
SCRATCH STYLE; The Carter Lick in 4/4 and 3/4; The Double Finger Scratch; Introducing the middle finger	44
ARPEGGIO STRUMS; In 3/4 and 4/4 time	54
TRAVIS PICKING; IN 3/4 and 4/4 time	57
MELODY PICKING; Filler strokes	62
RHYTHM PICKING;	77
CALYPSO	78
BLUES & JAZZ: Triplet Rhythm; Shuffle Rhythm; Double Thumbing; Rocker Strum; Syncopated Strum; Folk-Rock Strum.	81

ALPHABETICAL INDEX OF SONGS

TITLE	*PAGE*
A BICYCLE BUILT FOR TWO (Daisy Bell)	27
AMAZING GRACE	28
BATTLE HYMN OF THE REPUBLIC	70
BLUE TAIL FLY (JIMMY CRACK CORN) Three Versions	17, 18 & 19
BUFFALO GALS	12
CAMPTOWN RACES	43 & 69
CARELESS LOVE	32 & 82
CINDY	31
CLEMENTINE	66
CRAWDAD SONG, THE	51
DOWN BY THE RIVERSIDE	41
DOWN IN THE VALLEY	14 & 73
EVERYBODY LOVES SATURDAY NIGHT	80
FRERE JACQUES (BROTHER JOHN)	11
GO TELL AUNT RHODY	75
GREENSLEEVES	36
HE'S GOT THE WHOLE WORLD IN HIS HANDS	33 & 85
I LOVE THE MOUNTAINS	83
I'VE GOT PEACE LIKE A RIVER	38
JACOB'S LADDER	67
JOE TURNER	86
JUST A CLOSER WALK WITH THEE	88
L'IL LIZA JANE	23
LITTLE BROWN JUG	45
LONESOME VALLEY	72
MICHAEL, ROW THE BOAT ASHORE	59
NOBODY KNOWS THE TROUBLE I'VE SEEN	68
ONE MORE RIVER	24
ON TOP OF OLD SMOKEY	16
RED RIVER VALLEY	25
ROCK-A-MY-SOUL	91
ROW, ROW, ROW YOUR BOAT	65
SCARBOROUGH FAIR	55
SHE'LL BE COMIN' ROUND THE MOUNTAIN	53
SHE WORE A YELLOW RIBBON	48
SIDEWALKS OF NEW YORK, THE	49
STREETS OF LAREDO, THE	35
SWEET BETSY FROM PIKE	46
SWING LOW, SWEET CHARIOT	56
TAPS	65
THE MORE WE GET TOGETHER	58
THE SLOOP "JOHN B"	79
THIS LITTLE LIGHT OF MINE	90
THIS TRAIN	84
WHEN JOHNNY COMES MARCHING HOME	21
WHEN THE SAINTS GO MARCHING IN	40
WHEN YOU AND I WERE YOUNG, MAGGIE	61
WILDWOOD FLOWER	74

CARE OF THE AUTOHARP

Like any quality wooden instrument, your Autoharp is sensitive to heat and cold. Keep it away from sudden changes or extremes of temperature. It is best kept in a case, and can be wrapped in a towel within that case for further protection. Do not leave it in the sun, on a radiator or heating vent, by an open window, or in the trunk of your car.

And remember, the more you play your Autoharp, the mellower it will become, and the better it will stay in tune.

TUNING THE AUTOHARP

It is essential that you learn how to tune your Autoharp before beginning to play. Just one string that is too high or too low can throw off an entire melody and make you want to put the instrument away. Think of tuning—matching 36 strings to 36 pitches—as an exercise in ear training, and it will become a challenge, not a tedious task.

The best way to tune is by using a well-tuned piano, a cassette tuning tape,* or any instrument of fixed pitch such as a pitch pipe, xylophone, or resonator bell. You can tune chromatically, string by string, or diatonically, by scale steps, octaves, and chord intervals. The method you choose depends on your musical skill and knowledge of the instrument.

It is important to know that there is a great deal of stretch in new Autoharp strings. Therefore, the first few tunings will take longer and you will have to turn your wrench more than the usual 1/8 inch—all that is necessary in subsequent tunings, after the strings have settled.

Start by lifting each string individually and *gently stretching* it, as in fig. 1.

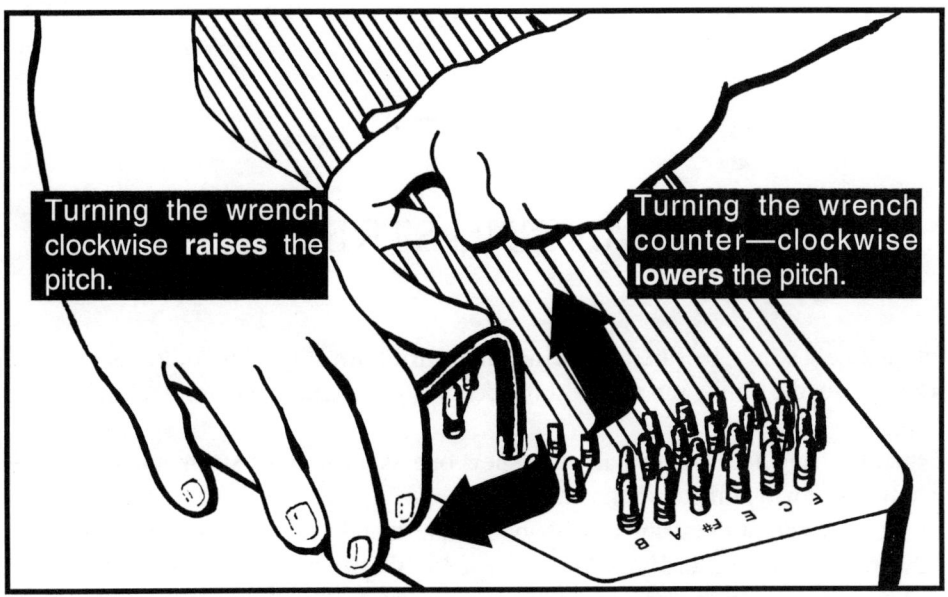

Figure 1

Turn the tuning wrench clockwise to raise the pitch and counterclockwise to lower it. After the string is up to pitch stretch it again and pluck it. In most cases it will have gone down in pitch. Repeat this process several times until the metal ball on the end of the string becomes tightly seated in the string anchor (see fig. 2, p.7), and the string stays in tune when stretched. Chromaharps and old "A" model Autoharps have a loop, not a ball, on the end of the string. (fig. 4, p.7)

Stay in Tune with Meg Peterson, 1979, demonstrates two different methods of tuning the Autoharp: beginning and advanced. Available from Meg Peterson, 33 South Pierson Rd., Maplewood, N.J. 07040.

When you have finished tuning, press each chord bar in turn and stroke heavily across all the strings. This will stretch them some more, and you will have to adjust the tuning accordingly. This first tuning may seem long and tedious, but, like any fine stringed instrument, the Autoharp must be tuned several times and played many hours before the tuning stabilizes.

Most standard 15 chord Autoharps have a scale label like the one in fig. 13, p.22. The label is a drawing of three octaves on the piano keyboard. The corresponding Autoharp string is shown directly above each key. Starting with the lowest string (the second F below middle C), place the tuning wrench securely on the corresponding tuning pin and pluck the string, turning the wrench very slowly—clockwise to raise the pitch, counterclockwise to lower it. Listen carefully to the fixed pitch you are using as a guide, and go up the scale, tuning and stretching each string in turn. Be sure you are matching the pitch in the proper octave and that your tuning wrench is placed securely on the pin of the string you are tuning—not the one next to it. Otherwise, you risk breaking a string!

For some people it is easier to hear the pitches in the middle octave than in the lower one. In this case, start on middle C (the 12th string from the bottom, or long side of the instrument), and go up the scale, tuning the middle octave first, and the higher and lower octaves last. After the middle octave is in tune, some of you may be able to match the higher and the lower to that octave. However, don't be discouraged if you can't. Beginners often find it difficult to differentiate between octaves (intervals eight tones apart), and are more comfortable with going up the scale chromatically, string by string.

After you have finished tuning, check your accuracy by pressing down each chord bar in succession, stroking across all the strings, and making any corrections as you listen to the chord intervals in sequence. The Autoharp, like the piano, is a tempered scale, so the same string used in several chords, even when perfectly in tune in one chord, may sound slightly sharp or flat in another. This will require only slight adjustments in pitch, however, and is hardly noticeable to the average ear.

Again, tuning your Autoharp is excellent ear training. Before long you will find that your pitch discrimination has greatly improved and you can identify any out-of-tune string just by pressing a chord and stroking across the strings.

CHANGING STRINGS

Before you put on a new string, be sure to **unwind the tuning pin** several revolutions by turning the wrench counterclockwise. Otherwise, the tuning pin will become deeply embedded in the pinblock when you start winding the new string up to pitch.

Next, remove the old string and slip the ball of the new one as far into the string anchor as it will go (Fig. 2). If you only slip it in halfway, it will pull out when you tighten the string. Remember, Chromaharps and old "A" model Autoharps have a loop on the end of the string that fits on a small metal peg, instead of into a string anchor (Fig.4).

Now slip the other end under the chord bars. Make sure it doesn't twist around the adjacent strings. Keep tension on the new string so it doesn't pop out of its anchor, as you insert about 1/2 inch of the wire into the small hole in the tuning pin.

As you turn the pin clockwise, be sure the end of the string is under the winding (fig. 3). This will prevent it from popping out. Continue to keep the string taut as you wind, pressing down with your index finger to keep the end of the string in place.

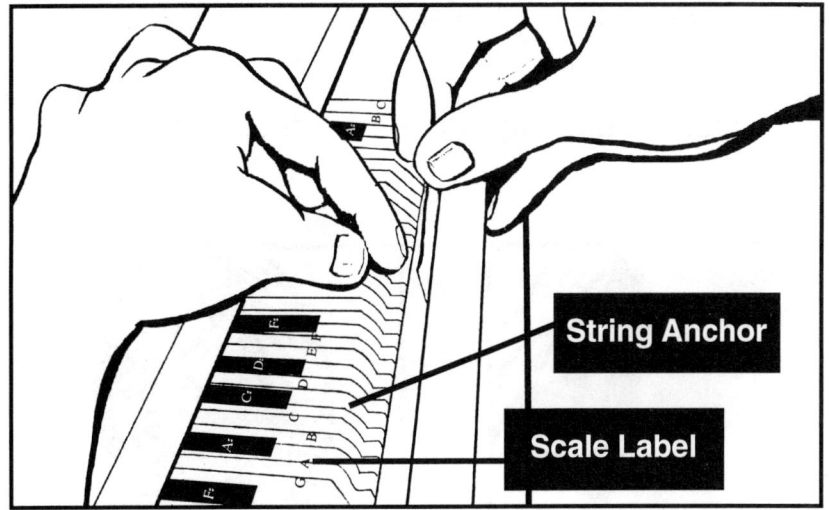
Autoharp string with a metal ball at the end, being inserted into the string anchor.

Figure 3
Winding on a new string.

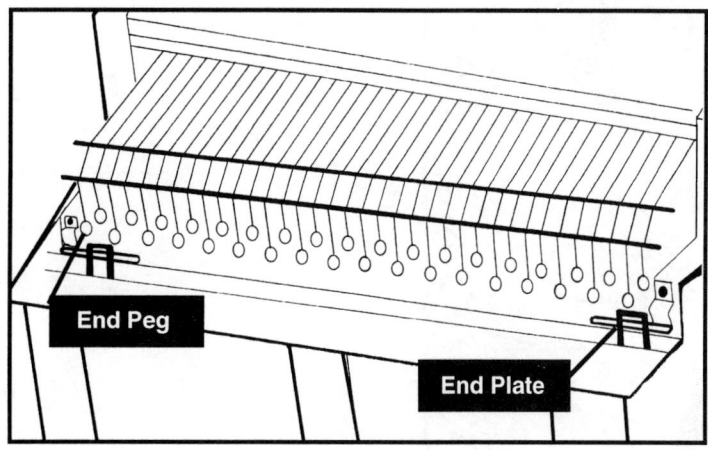

Figure 4
Chromaharp strings have a loop which fits over the end peg.
The end plate snaps open for convenience in changing strings.

HOW TO HOLD THE AUTOHARP

Most beginning players put the Autoharp:

on the table   or   on the lap

Figure 5

Figure 6

*Note the angle of the instruments in relation to the player's body.

Figure 7
More advanced players hold it in their arms Appalachian style.

CHOOSING A PICK

Here are some common types of picks used by Autoharp players.

Plastic thumb pick

Plastic and metal finger picks

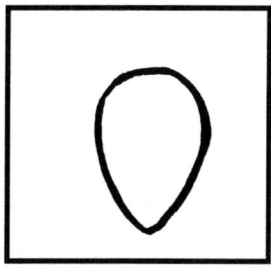

Flat plastic pick

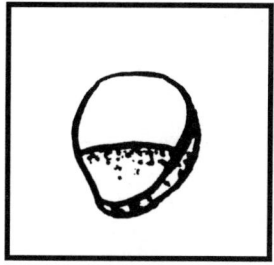

Felt pick

Most players use a plastic thumb pick and metal finger picks. Figure 8 shows the correct way to wear metal finger picks, and fig. 9 shows how to wear plastic finger picks. Both figures show the player wearing a plastic thumb pick..

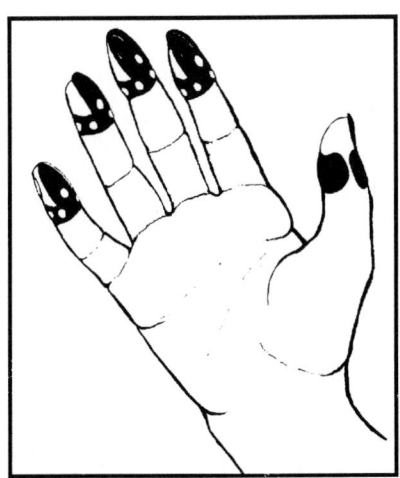

Figure 8

This is the correct way to wear finger picks.

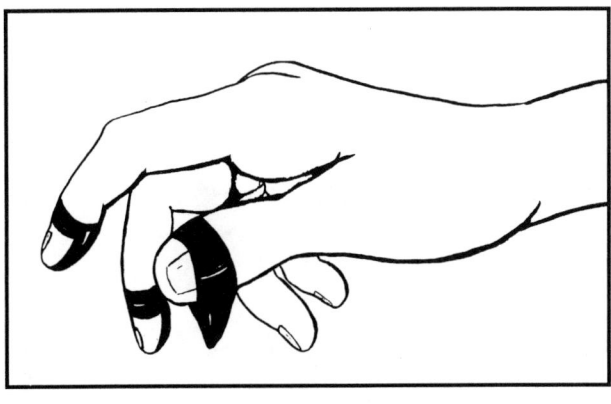

Figure 9

Picks should fit snugly .

These picks come in many different sizes and gauges. Select one that fits snugly so it won't twist or come off as you play. Plastic picks can be heated in boiling water and molded to fit the finger. And the point of the thumb pick can be filed and rounded off to execute fast strums more smoothly.

The letter designations, **T, i**, and **m** stand for **thumb, index finger**, and **middle finger**, and are used throughout this book to explain various strum patterns. Later on, as you become more advanced in your technique, all five fingers will be used.

HOW TO STROKE THE AUTOHARP

Do not confuse the words "stroke" and "strum." A **stroke** is a single motion across one or more sections of the Autoharp. A **strum** is made up of several strokes combined in a rhythmic pattern.

> An upstoke goes from the lower (bass) to the higher (treble) strings and away from the body.
> A downstroke comes from the higher down to the lower stings, toward the body.

Since you will use only upstrokes with the thumb in the next several songs—with or without a pick—there will be no arrows, only slash marks. Each of these marks (/) will represent a repetition of the stroke.

YOU ARE NOW READY TO PLAY

Place the Autoharp on your lap or on a table and press the C chord down firmly with your left index finger. Use the thumb of your right hand to stroke all the way across the strings:

To the right of the chord bars.   OR   To the left about two inches from the chord bars.

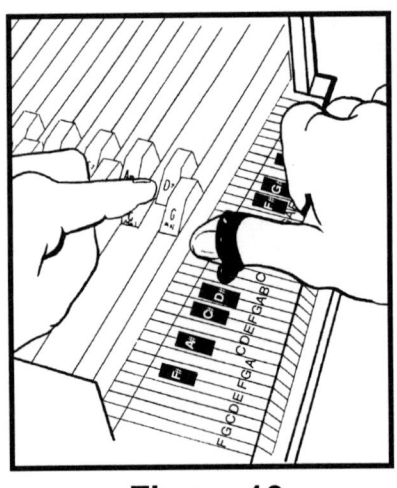

Figure 10

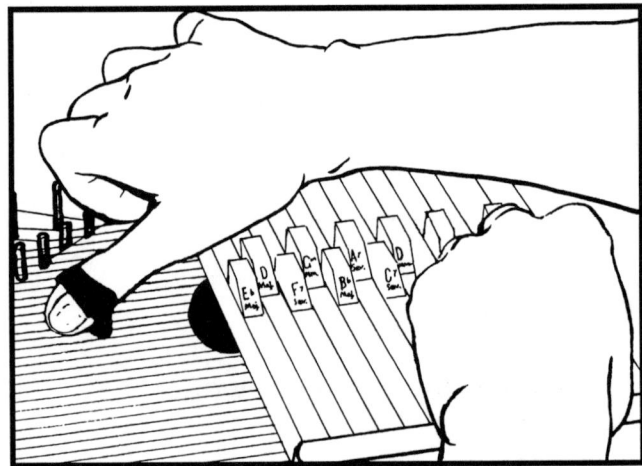

Figure 11

Fig. 11 requires you to cross your right hand over your left, but the tone produced is much more mellow. The right side is most often reserved for special effects or a more "twangy" kind of country playing.

If you are left-handed, no crossover will be necessary. Just press the chord bar down with your right index finger and stroke the strings to the left of the chord bars with your left thumb.

Now, stroke the strings several times all the way across, being sure to **press only one chord at a time,** holding it down firmly while stroking. Use a sweeping motion, making the instrument ring. The right elbow should be slightly elevated and the wrist flexible. Stroke fairly rapidly to get the full effect of the chord. When done properly the strings will continue to "sing." But if you stroke too heavily the sound will be dull and scratchy.

This first song requires only one chord. Press down the chord bar marked C Maj., written above the music as C. Repeat the stroke every time you see a slash (/). Remember, as you begin you'll use only upstrokes. Count 1, 2, 3, 4, keeping a steady beat and matching the strokes to the music, playing only on the 1st and 3rd beats of the measure.

This pattern of two strokes per measure is repeated throughout the song.

FRERE JACQUES

(Brother John)

Chords Used: C

Old French Round

> In this book, the chord or chords used in each song are indicated on the left above the music. Always find the location of the chords before beginning the song.

CHANGING CHORDS

The next song has two chords. In order to make a smooth transition from one chord to another, you must be sure to press the chord bar down and stroke the strings at exactly the same time. If you press a second chord before beginning the stroke, it will muffle the sound of the previous one and your playing will be unmusical and choppy. Before you begin, try pressing down and stroking the C chord, then changing to the G7, then back to the C, until you have a clear, seamless transition.

You can use the index finger on the C and the middle finger on the G7.

BUFFALO GALS

Chords Used: C & G7

Traditional

You have now played two songs in 4/4 time, counting "1, 2, 3, 4" and playing two strokes to the measure. The following information will help you understand the basic time signatures:

4/4 = Common (four-quarter) Time: 4 strokes or beats to the measure, or 2 strokes, on the 1st & 3rd beats.

Press the C chord and stroke in a steady beat, counting "1, 2, 3, 4" as you play. Each slash (/) mark means to repeat the stroke. The accent mark (>) at the beginning of each measure means to emphasize that stroke as you practice.

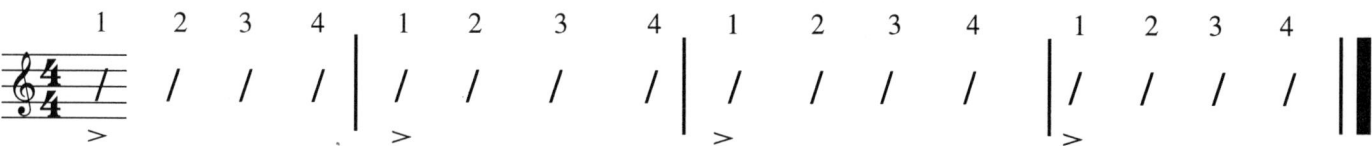

2/4 = Two Four (two quarter) Time: 2 strokes or beats to the measure (this is also called March Time).
Press the C chord and stroke in the following manner, counting "1, 2, 1, 2" as you play, and slightly emphasizing the first stroke of each measure.

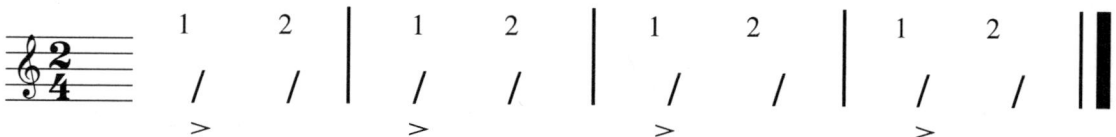

3/4 = Three-four (three-quarter) Time: 3 strokes or beats to the measure (this is also called Waltz Time)
Press the C chord and count "1, 2, 3 1, 2, 3" as you play, accenting (>) the first beat in each measure.

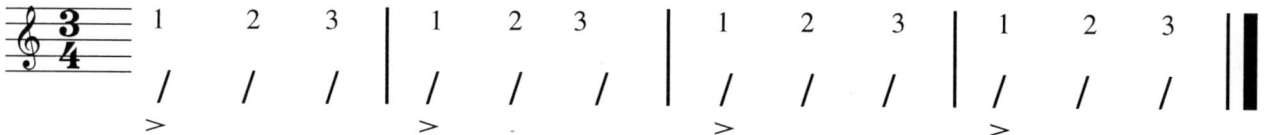

Two More Rhythm Symbols

C means the same as 4/4 time. ¢ is played the same as 2/2 or a fast 4/4. Count "1 & 2 &" instead of "1, 2, 3, 4."

This next song is in 3/4 time, so you will count in three instead of in four, playing three strokes to a measure. Notice that you will use the same two chords as in the previous song. Each slash mark (/) means to continue stroking the same chord until a new one appears above the music. Listen to the harmonies as you sing, and you will soon begin to hear for yourself when to change the chord.

DOWN IN THE VALLEY

Chords Used: C & G7

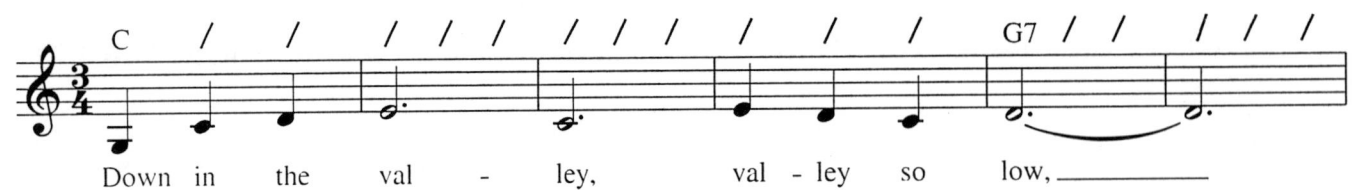
Down in the val-ley, val-ley so low,

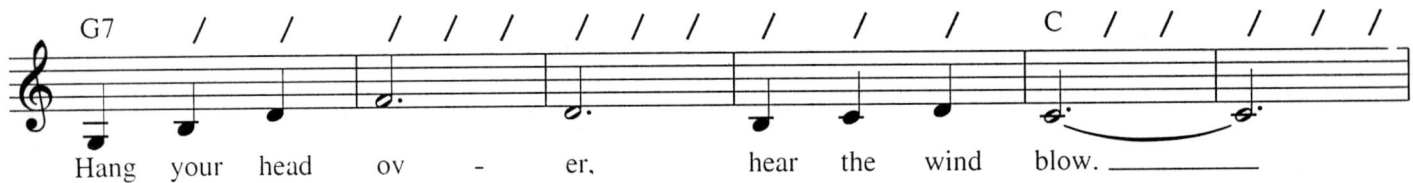
Hang your head ov-er, hear the wind blow.

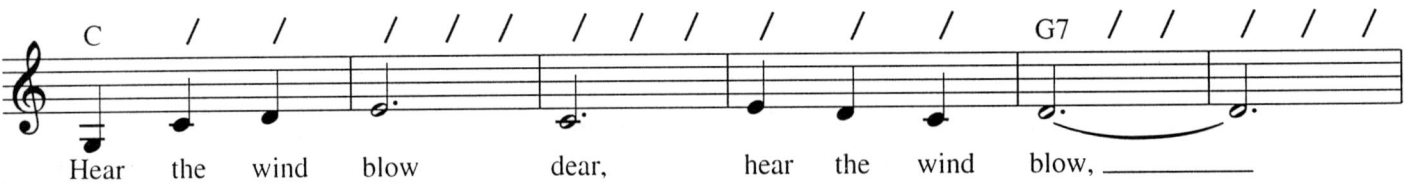
Hear the wind blow dear, hear the wind blow,

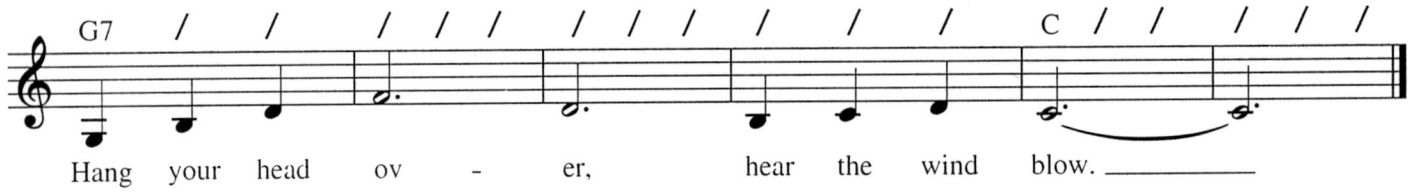
Hang your head ov-er, hear the wind blow.

2. Roses love sunshine, violets love dew;
   Angels in heaven know I love you.
   Know I love you, dear, Know I love you.
   Angels in heaven know I love you.

3. Send me a letter, send it by mail;
   Send it in care of the Birmingham jail,
   Birmingham jail, dear, Birmingham jail,
   Send it in care of the Birmingham jail.

FINGERING

There are no set rules for Autoharp fingering. However, for most simple tunes, the **index, middle, and ring fingers** are placed on the three principal chords in a particular key, especially when the Autoharp is played on a table or on your lap. As you can see in fig.12, the index finger is placed on the C chord, the middle finger on the G7, and the ring finger on the F, the three principal chords in the key of C. Naturally, when the Autoharp is picked up and played Appalachian style as on p.42, this fingering will be reversed and, depending on the arrangement of the chords on a particular model, you may want to use only one or two fingers, or even your thumb and little finger to execute difficult stretches.

Ultimately you must experiment and come up with the fingering that works best for you, using the fingers that are strongest and can hold the chords down the most effectively for your style of playing.

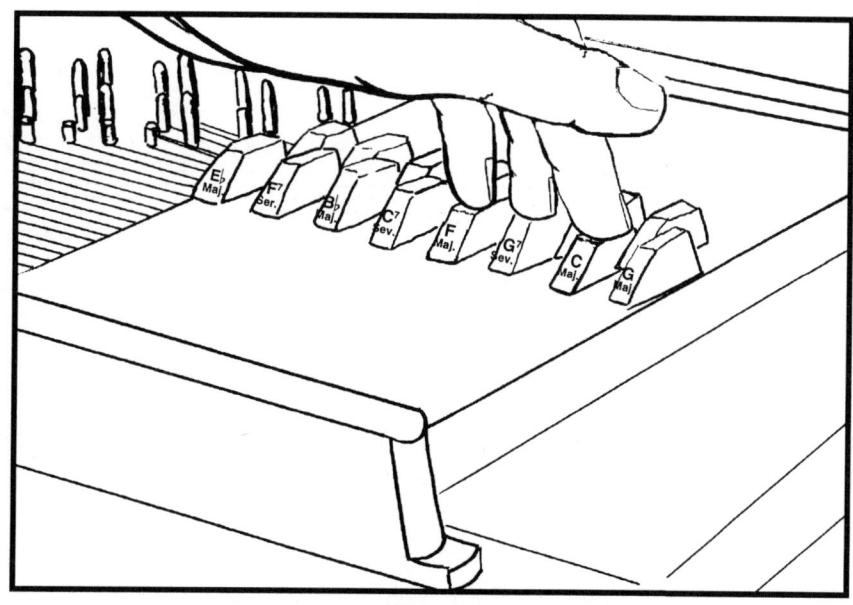

Figure 12
Finger Position

Practice changing chords in the key of C, using the above fingering. Press each chord in turn, C, F, G7, and back to C, until you are familiar with their locations and can change chords and stroke simultaneously.

You are now ready to play another 3/4 time song, using three chords instead of two. Be sure your plastic thumb pick is secure and you stroke the strings in a firm, gentle motion, letting each chord ring.

ON TOP OF OLD SMOKY

Chords Used: C, F, & G7

Key of C
C, F, & G7

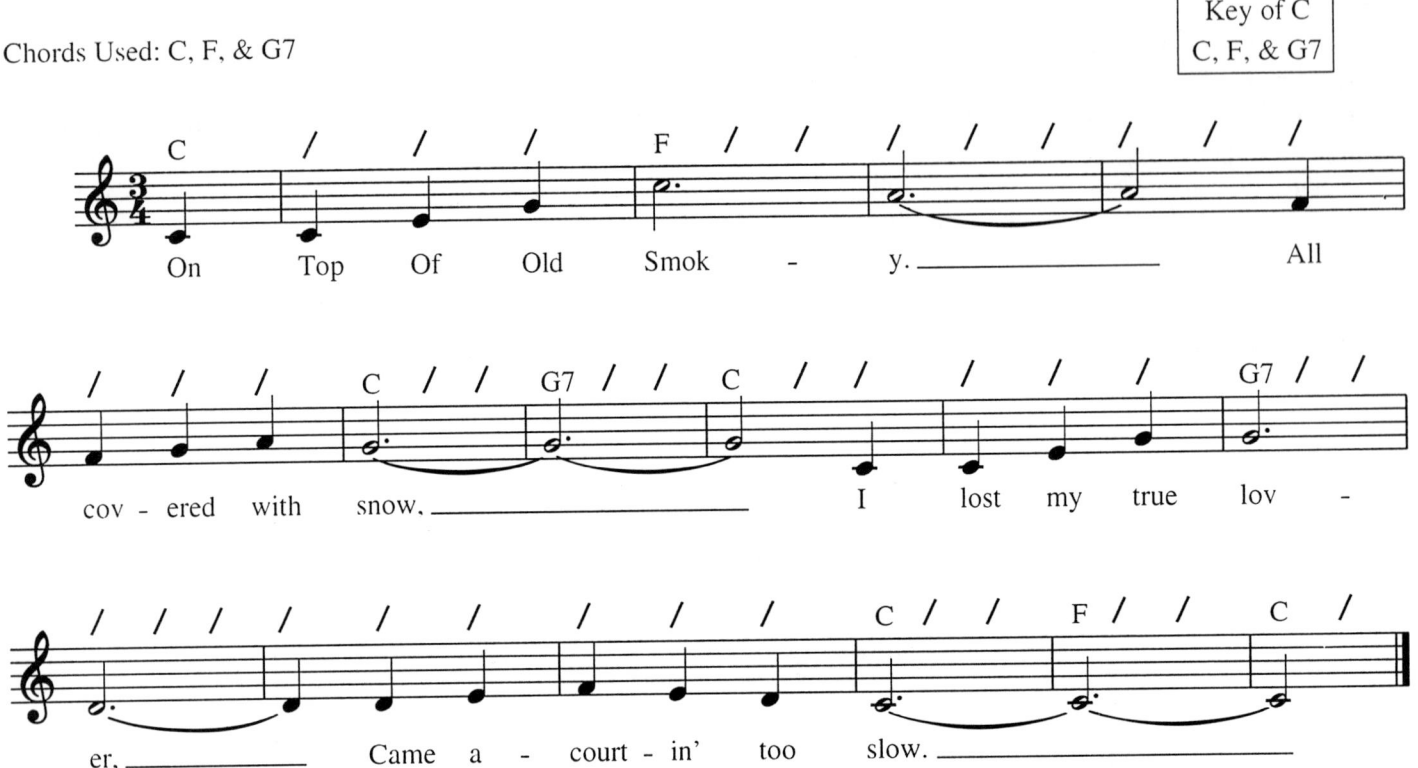

2. For courtin's a pleasure, and partin's a grief,
   And a false-hearted lover is worse than a thief.

3. For a thief, he will rob you and take what you have,
   But a false-hearted lover will put you in your grave.

As you practiced stroking the three chords in the key of C, you probably noticed that they have a certain harmonic relationship to one another. They sound good together. This same relationship is found in every key on the Autoharp.

To help you understand this, a Roman numeral is assigned to the three principal chords—I, IV, or V7—of each key. Once you have learned which chords go together in each key, and their "sound" is familiar to you, you will be able to play numerous songs by ear.

For example: the next song introduces you to three new keys: G, F, and D. Before you begin each version, play the three main chords of the key as shown above the music, and listen to how they sound together—just as you did in the key of C.

First, start with the key of G, and play G (I), C (IV), and D7 (V7), returning to G (I). Repeat this, until you are familiar with the location of the chords and how they sound in sequence. Now play "Blue Tail Fly," stroking twice in every measure.

BLUE-TAIL FLY

(Jimmy Crack Corn)

Chords Used: G, C, & D7

Key of G
G, C, & D7

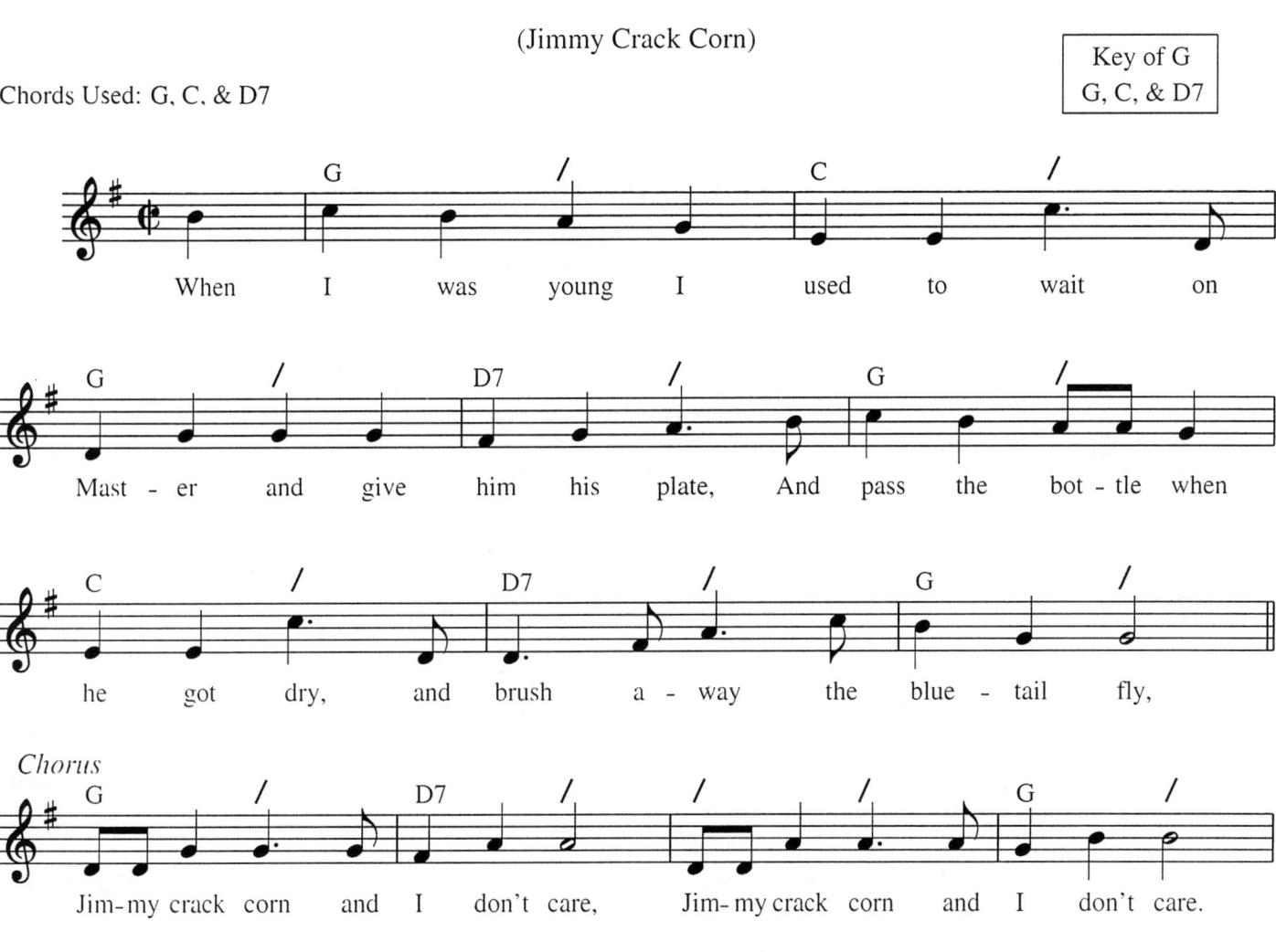

2. One day he rode around the farm,
   The flies so num-'rous they did swarm:
   One chanced to bite him on the thigh,
   The devil take the blue-tail fly.
       Jimmy crack corn etc.

3. The pony ran, he jumped and pitched,
   He threw old master in the ditch.
   He died, the jury wondered why,
   The verdict was, the blue-tail fly.
       Jimmy crack corn etc.

4. They laid him underneath a tree
   His epitaph for all to see:
   "Beneath this stone, I'm forced to lie,
   A victim of the blue-tail fly."
       Jimmy crack corn etc.

Now, play "Blue-Tail Fly" in the key of F. Place the index finger on the F (I) chord, the ring finger on the B♭ (IV) chord, and the middle finger on the C7 (V7) chord, and practice the chord changes in that order, returning to the F (I) chord.

The fingering for playing "Blue-Tail Fly" in the key of G and F is the same as in fig. 12, p.15. When you play in the key of D, however, it's quite different, due to the location of the chords on the Autoharp. You may want to use your middle finger on the D, your index finger on the G and your ring finger on the A7, depending on the size of your hand. But you must really decide for yourself what is most comfortable.

Now play D (I), G (IV), A7 (V7), and D (I) several times in sequence before starting the song, noticing again the sound relationship of the three principal chords to one another.

BLUE-TAIL FLY
(Jimmy Crack Corn)

Key of D
D, G, & A7

Chords Used: D, G, & A7

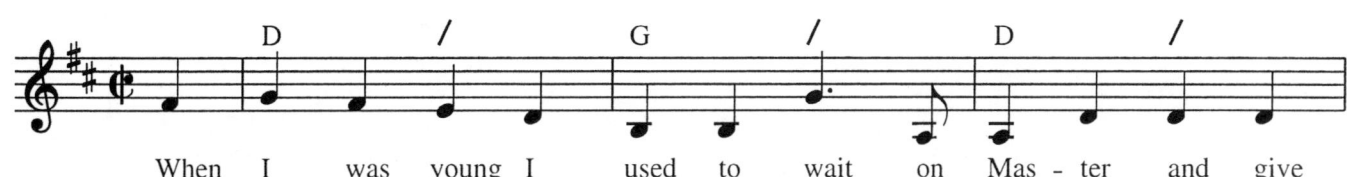

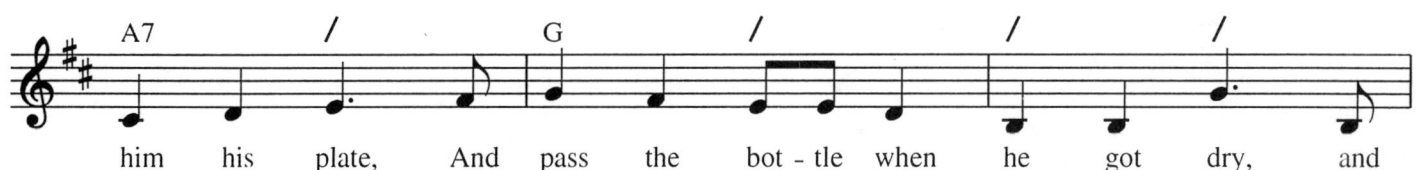

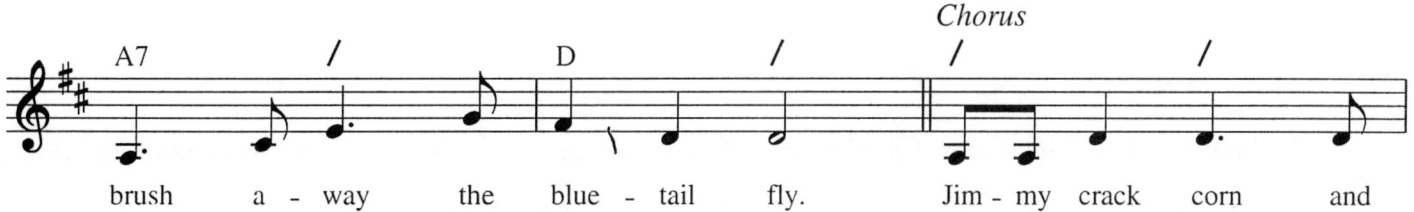

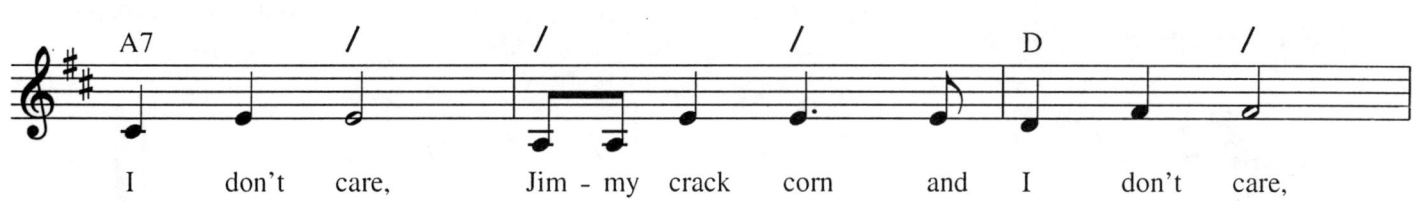

As you played this song in three different keys, you probably noticed that one of them accommodated your singing range better than the other two. Or you may have felt that the song sounded better in one key than in another. That's why it's good to learn these different chord groupings. Soon you'll be able to take simple melodies and transpose (change) them from one key to the other by ear, just knowing the I, IV, and V7 chords in each key.

Right now try playing "Blue-Tail Fly" in C (I), F (IV), and G7 (V7), and listening for the chord changes by ear.

Here is a simple chart to guide you in playing in the different keys available on the 15 chord Autoharp.

Key	Principal Chords		
	I chord	IV chord	V 7 chord
C Maj.	C	F	G7
G Maj.	G	C	D7
F Maj.	F	B♭	C7
D Maj.	D	G	A7
A min.	A Min.	D Min.	E7
D Min.	D Min.	G Min.	A7

*For further study of the chord groupings available on the Autoharp, and how to transpose, see p. 161, *The Complete Method,* and p. 33, *Let's Play the Autoharp.*

So far, all the songs you've played are in major keys. Now try one in A minor. It introduces a new time (key) signature.

6/8 = Compound (six-eight) time: 6 strokes or beats to the measure, or 2 strokes, on the 1st and the 4th beats

When used on slow songs, such as "Greensleeves" (p.36), 6/8 time is organized into sets of six beats with a primary accent on the 1st beat and a secondary accent on the 4th. Count "1, 2, 3, 4, 5, 6" as you practice, accenting the stroke on the count of 1 and 4.

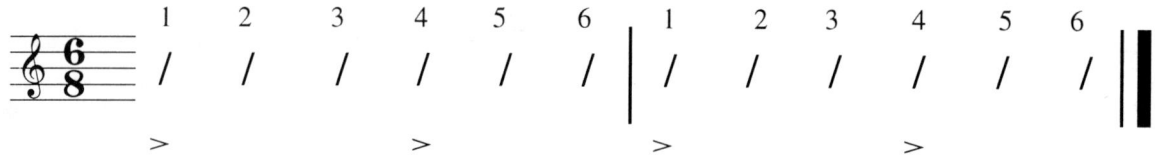

For faster songs like "One More River"(p.24) and "When Johnny Comes Marching Home," you will feel only two beats to a measure. Instead of counting out six short beats, count "1, 2, 1, 2," stroking only on the 1st and the 4th beat. The slash marks will tell you when to stroke.

Notice the difference in mood as this haunting melody moves from a minor key to a major key several times throughout the song. Be sure to locate the new chords, A min. and E7, and find a comfortable fingering before beginning to play.

WHEN JOHNNY COMES MARCHING HOME

Chords Used: Am, C, G, & E7

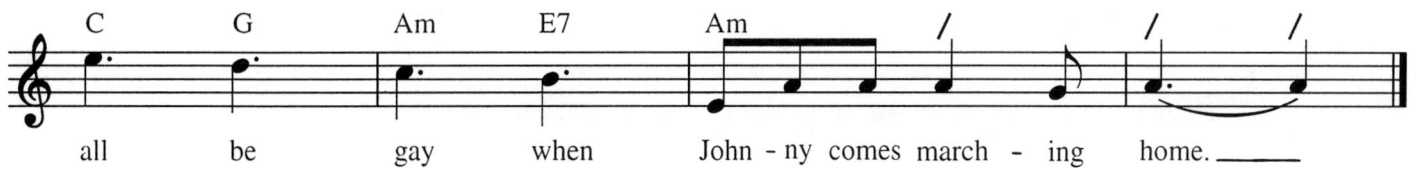

SIMPLE BACK-UP STRUMS

A **strum** is a series of strokes played in one or more octaves of the Autoharp in a rhythmic pattern. Strums can be played with the thumb alone, or with the thumb and one or more fingers. They can be all up strokes, or a combination of up and down strokes. As you played the previous songs you probably didn't stroke all the way across the strings, but varied your strokes to make them more interesting—producing just such a pattern.

In order to understand these strum patterns, look at the scale label in fig. 13. It shows the three octaves, or sections, of the Autoharp—**the lower, middle and higher**—and the symbols used to indicate a stroke in each one. These octaves are approximate areas only. You need not stroke across the entire octave, nor be rigid about the number of strings sounded.

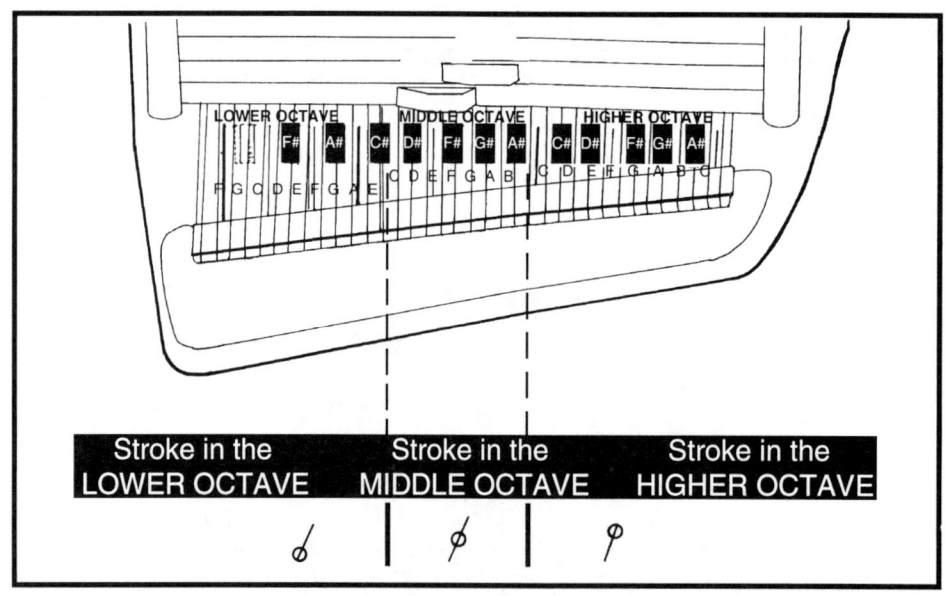

Figure 13
Scale Label with Octave Designations

Arrows are placed on the above stroke symbols to indicate the direction of the stroke:

↗ = An **upstroke**, played from the lower (bass) to the higher (treble) strings. (If the Autoharp is on your lap or the table, the stroke would be away from your body.)
↙ = A **downstroke**, played from the higher to the lower strings, toward your body.

Let's begin with Strum #1, an upstroke in the lower octave followed by a short upstroke in the middle octave. The letter "T" means to use the thumb—with or without a pick.

As you practice, it helps to count aloud, then recite the octave designations like this:

one	two	three	four
lower	middle	lower	middle

Press the C chord and repeat this several times, like a chant, as you practice the strum. The same procedure is used in learning all subsequent strums.

Strum #1

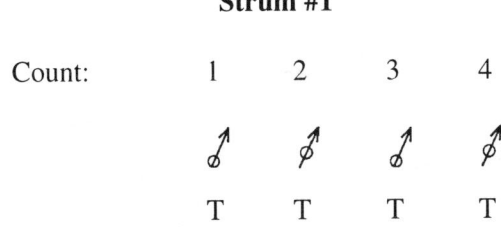

The strum pattern is placed over the first few measures of the music, but should be continued throughout the song.

You'll recognize the chords used in this piece as the three principal chords in the key of C. Be sure to keep the strum pattern going, even when there's a chord change in the middle of it—as in measures 3, 7, 10, 11, 14, and 15.

L'IL LIZA JANE

Chords Used: C, F, & G7   Traditional

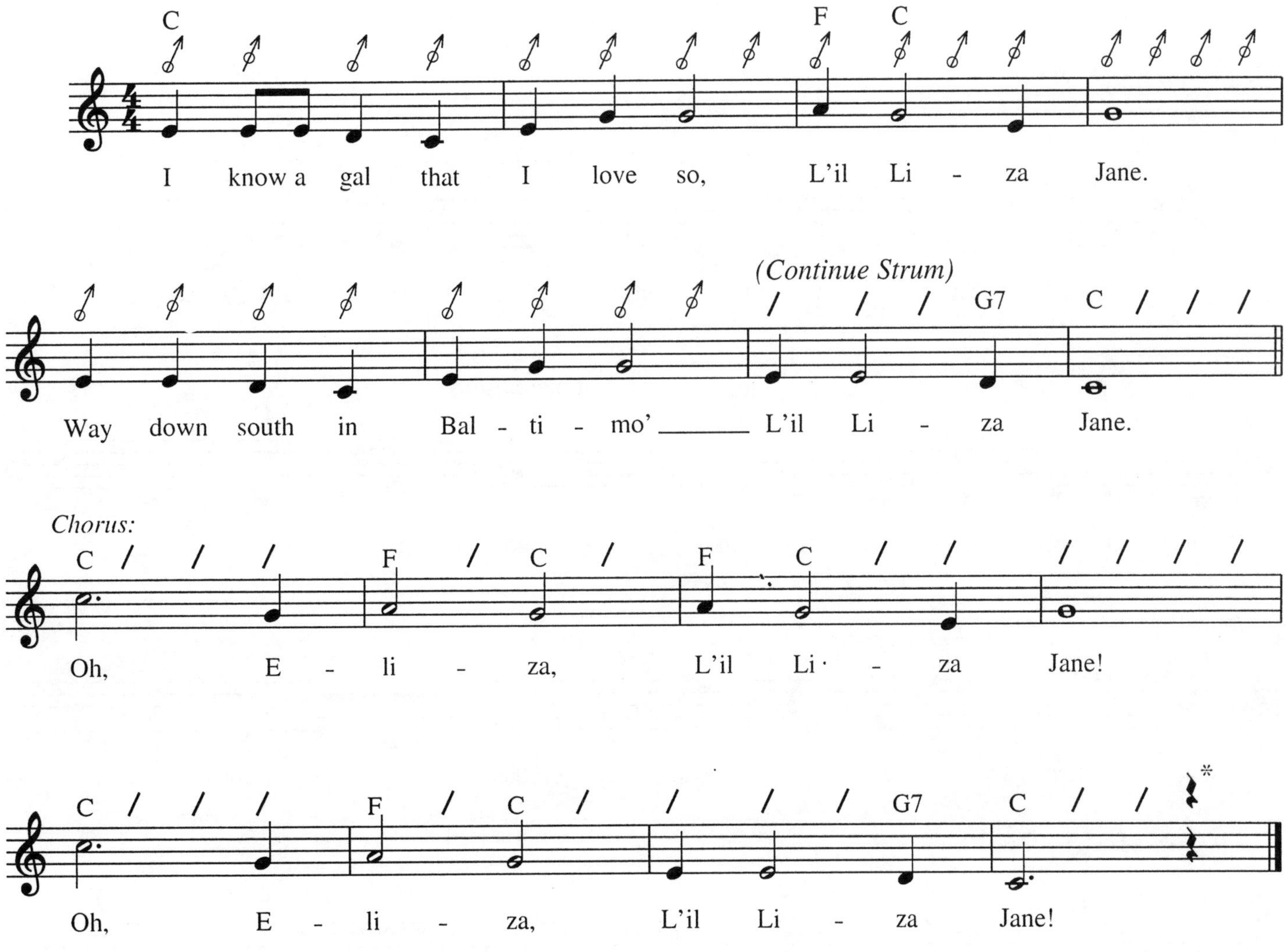

I know a gal that I love so, L'il Li - za Jane.

Way down south in Bal - ti - mo' ____ L'il Li - za Jane.

Chorus:

Oh, E - li - za, L'il Li - za Jane!

Oh, E - li - za, L'il Li - za Jane!

* 𝄽 = to rest for one beat

The next strum is a 6/8 variation of Strum #1 with only two strokes to the measure. It starts with an accented upstroke in the lower octave on the 1st beat and a stroke in the middle octave on the 4th beat. Because the tempo is fast you will feel only two beats to the measure, as you did in "When Johnny Comes Marching Home," p.21. Note that it also uses the three principal chords in the key of C.

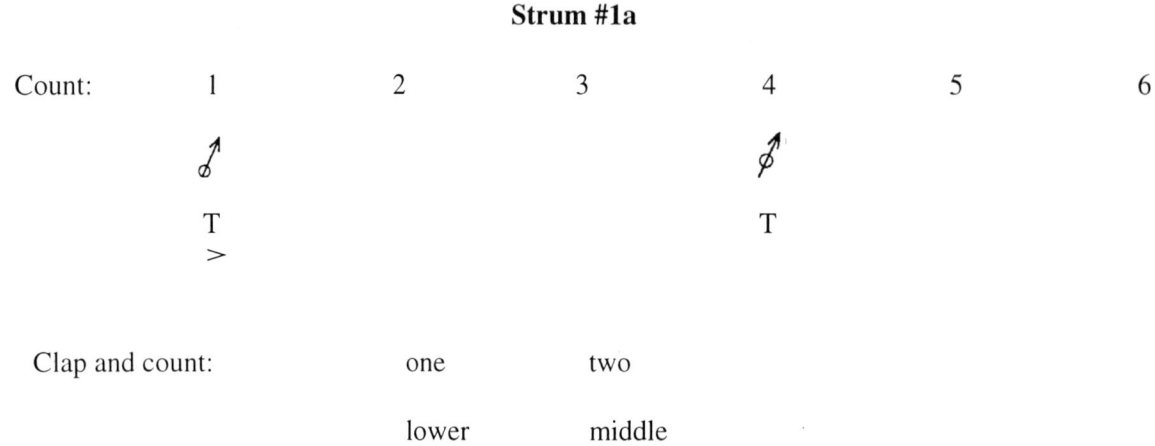

For variety and a brighter sound, play the second stroke of the pattern in the higher, rather than the middle octave.

ONE MORE RIVER

Chords Used: C, F, & G7

Spiritual

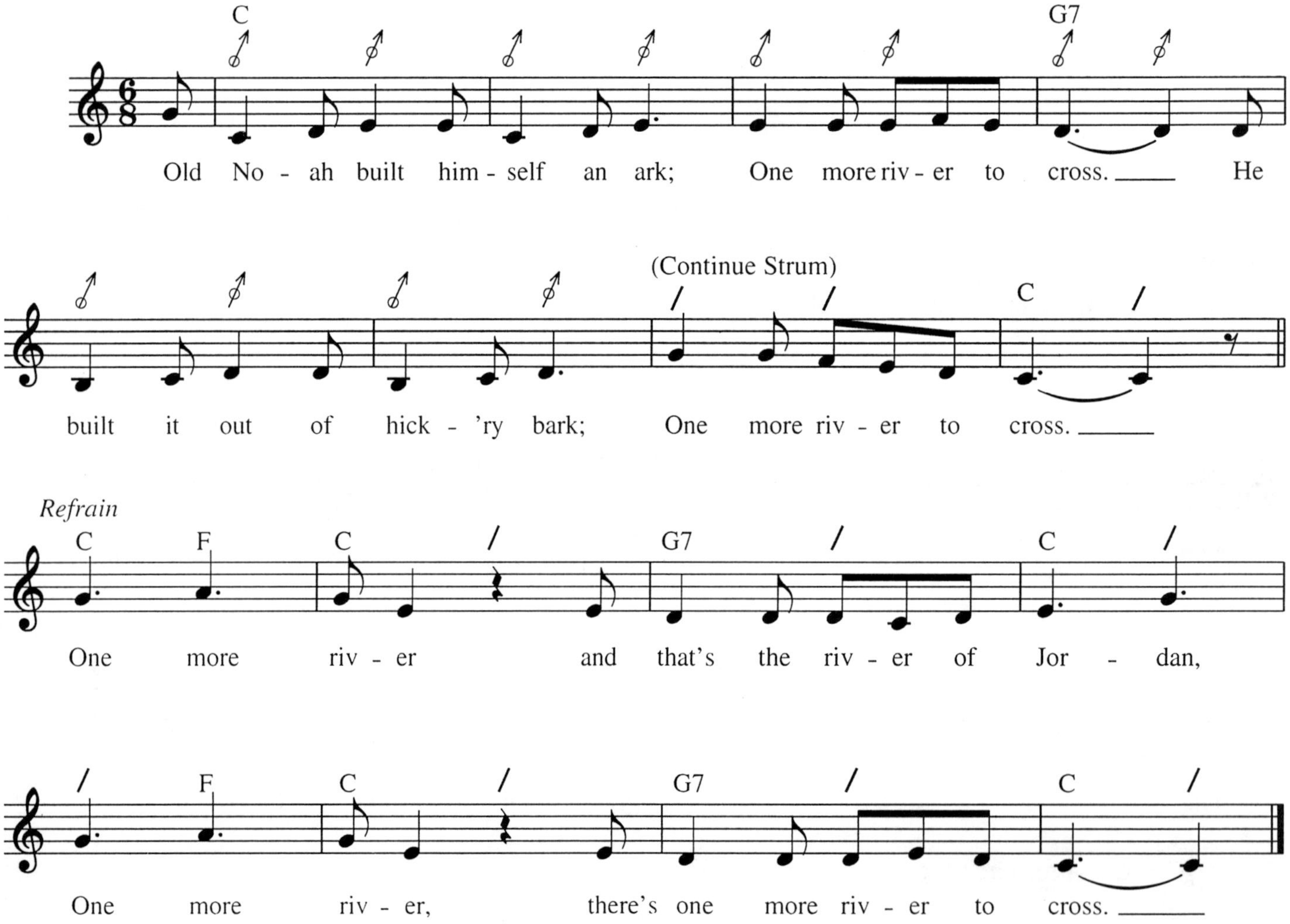

Now let's try a strum using all three octaves of the Autoharp.

Strum #2

Count: 1   2   3   4

T   T   T   T
>

Play the pattern slowly several times, counting the beats and repeating the octave names as you did before:

one   two   three   four

lower   middle   higher   middle

Once you are comfortable with the three octaves, you can shorten your strokes and increase your tempo (speed). Notice that you automatically emphasize the first stroke of every pattern (>), which is like the bass beat of a guitar accompaniment. To make the strum more interesting, you can vary the initial beat, hitting the very lowest strings on the first pattern, and moving up several strings to start the second. Both strokes will still be in the lower octave.

This next song uses the three principal chords in the key of F, plus an F7, which is added for harmonic richness.

RED RIVER VALLEY

Chords Used: F, B♭, C7, & F7

Chorus:
(No Chords) F — C7 — F
Come and sit by my side if you love me,

(Continue Strum) — C7
Do not has-ten to bid me a-dieu,

F — F7 — B♭
But re-mem-ber the Red Riv-er Val-ley,

C7 — F
And the cow-boy that loves you so true.

Verse: From this valley they say you are go–ing,
We will miss your bright eyes and sweet smile.
For they say you are tak–ing the sun–shine.
That has bright–ened our path–way a while.

(Chorus)

Strum #3

Count: 1   2   3

         ♩   ♪   ♪

         T   T   T
         >

This next strum is in 3/4 and is played with an accented upstroke in the lower octave and two short, crisp upstrokes in the higher. It's the typical "oom-pah-pah" rhythm used in old-time music halls, and gives a twangy resonance to this popular old tune. When you've learned the strum, try varying it by using the lower and middle octaves instead of the lower and higher, and see which one you like the best. You can also use an alternating bass stroke to add variety and depth. Repeat to yourself as you practice in a slow waltz tempo:

one   two   three

lower   higher   higher

A Bicycle Built for Two

(Daisy Bell)

Chords Used: F, B♭, C7, Dm, G7, F7

Words and Music by
Harry Dacre

Now, let's try another strum in 3/4 time using all three octaves.

Strum #4

Count: 1   2   3

T   T   T

Before you play this familiar old hymn, practice stroking and counting in each of the three octaves like this:

one   two   three

lower   middle   higher

AMAZING GRACE

Chords Used: F, B♭, C7, & Dm

2. 'Twas grace that taught my heart to fear,
   And grace my fears relieved;
   How precious did that grace appear,
   The hour I first believed!

3. Through many dangers, toils and snares
   I have already come;
   'Tis grace hath brought me safe thus far,
   And grace will lead me home.

4. When we've been there ten thousand years,
   Bright shining as the sun,
   We've no less days to sing God's praise
   Than when we first begun.

5. Alleluia, Alleluia, Alleluia, Praise God! (Repeat)

COMBINING UP AND DOWN STROKES

All the strokes you've played so far have been upstrokes with the thumb in one or more octaves of the Autoharp. Now it's time to introduce the downstroke—still using the thumb.

Strum #5

Count:	1	2	3	4	&
	↑	↑	↑	↑	↓
	T	T	T	T	T

This pattern is similar to Strum #2 on p.25, except that there are two strokes in the middle octave on the fourth beat instead of just one. Clap your hands to the beat, add the direction of the strokes as well as the octave designations, and repeat aloud:

one	two	three	four - and
lower	middle	higher	mid - dle
up	up	up	up - down

Now play the strum on the Autoharp in the rhythm you just clapped. Notice that the two strokes on the fourth beat ("four-and") are played twice as fast as the other three strokes.

This fast up and down pattern is important, because it lays the foundation for all mountain and country strums. Start practicing slowly at first, then speed up, using a rotating wrist. Do not wiggle your thumb, but keep it firm. This is a wrist, not a finger action.

Notice how the strokes become shorter as the tempo increases. Do not drag the thumb along the strings heavily, but lightly stroke only a few strings at a time.

CINDY

Chords Used: D, G, & A7

3. I wish I had a needle,
   As fine as I could sew;
   I'd sew the girls to my coattail,
   And down the road I'd go...
   Chorus: Get along, etc.

INTRODUCING THE INDEX FINGER

Strum #5a is a variation of the previous strum, using the index finger instead of the thumb on the final down stroke. Wear a finger pick as in fig. 8, p.9. Learning this fast alternating thumb-index finger pattern will help prepare you for the filler strokes used in advanced Appalachian and country picking.

* The strum—counted the same as #5—looks like this:

Strum #5a

Count:	1	2	3	4	&
	♩	♩	♩	♩	♩
	T	T	T	T	i**

**i=a stroke with the index finger

The more frequent chord changes in measures 5, 6, 9, and 12 of "Careless Love" bring out the melody. Practice these changes, first, by stroking all the way across the strings, then incorporate them into the strum. Be sure to keep the strum pattern going over the chord changes.

CARELESS LOVE

Chords Used: C, F, G7, & C7

Traditional folk

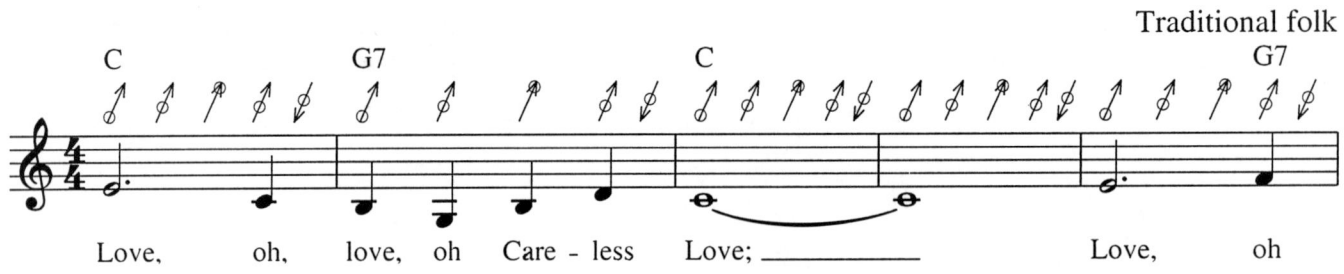

Love, oh, love, oh Care - less Love; _____ Love, oh

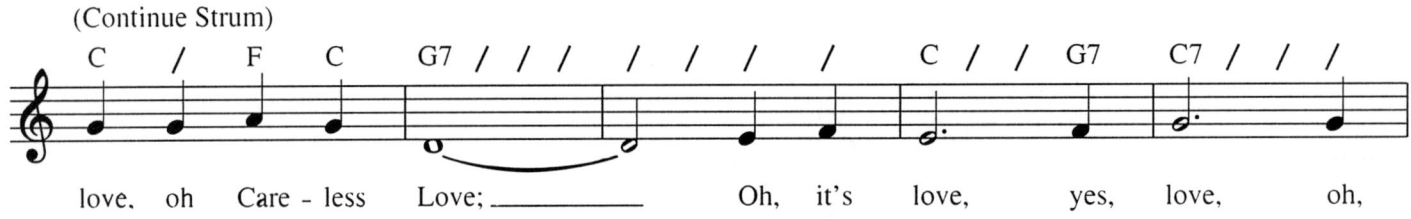

love, oh Care - less Love; _____ Oh, it's love, yes, love, oh,

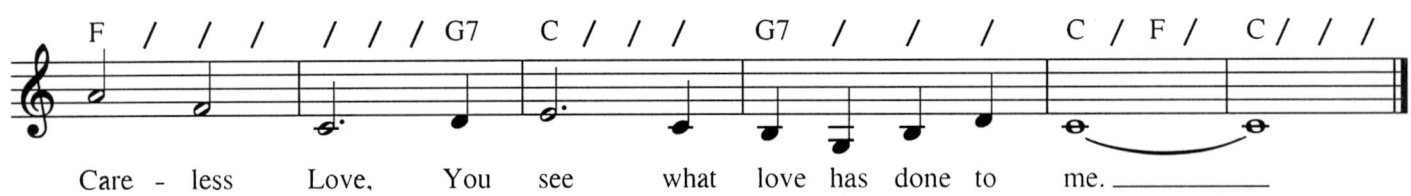

Care - less Love, You see what love has done to me. _____

*Mel Bay's Complete Book of Traditional and Country Autoharp Picking Styles by Meg Peterson, Mel Bay Publications, Inc., 1986. Study of filler strokes, pp. 59-84.

2. I cried last night and the night before, *(3 x)*
   Gonna cry tonight and cry no more.

3. I love my momma and my poppa too, *(3 x)*
   But I'd leave them both to go with you.

4. When I wore an apron low, *(3 x)*
   You'd follow me through rain and snow.

5. Now I wear my apron high, *(3 x)*
   You see my door and pass on by.

6. How I wish that train would come, *(3 x)*
   And take me back where I come from.

Just for fun, vary Strum #5a by counting the fourth beat "4 and uh," which will give this next tune a jazzy, folk-rock sound.

Put an accent on the "uh," add the finger designations, and count the whole pattern like this:

one	two	three	four	- and -	uh
thumb	thumb	thumb	thumb		index
up	up	up	up		down

HE'S GOT THE WHOLE WORLD IN HIS HANDS

Chords Used: C & G7   Traditional

Repeat the verses three times, ending with "He's Got The Whole World In His Hands."

2. He's got the little bitty baby in His hands...

3. He's got you and me brother in His hands...

4. He's got all of Creation in His hands...

5. He's got the wind and the rain in his hands...

THE ARPEGGIANDO STROKE

This is a gentle stroke played slowly up and down two or more octaves on the Autoharp.

The upstroke (away from the body) looks like this:

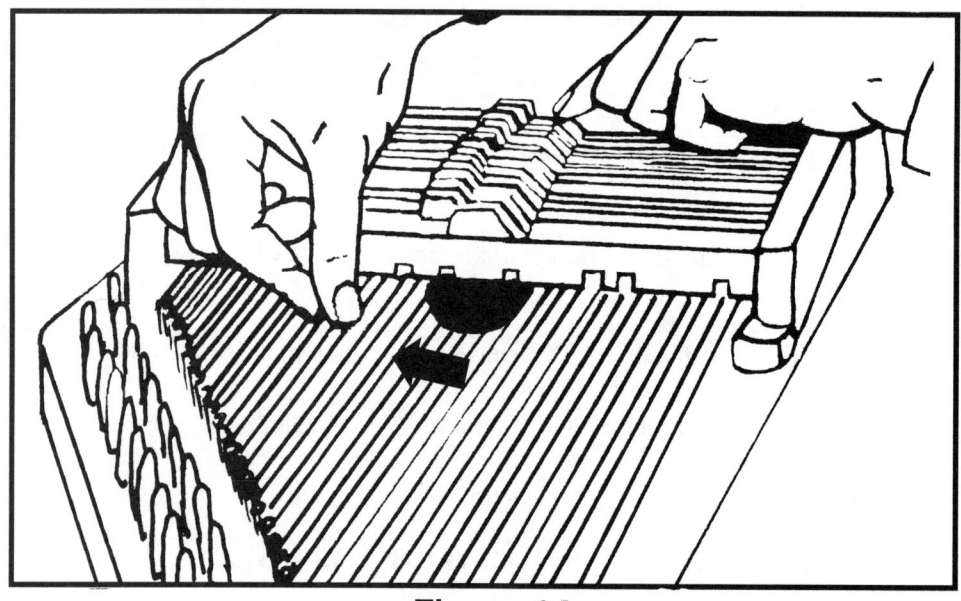

Figure 14

The sign for an upstroke is: ↗

The downstroke (toward the body) looks like this:

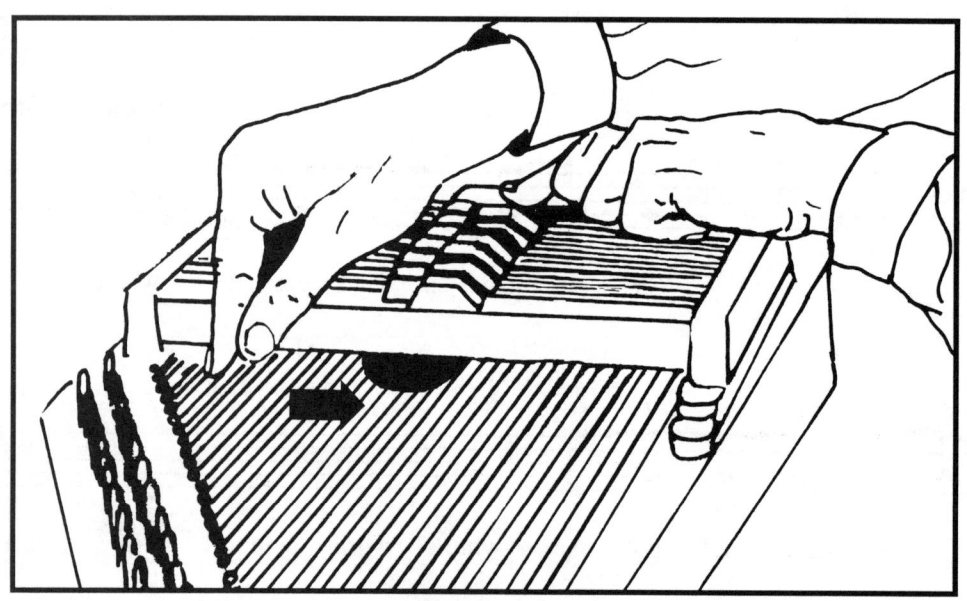

Figure 15

The sign for a downstroke is: ↙

The arpeggiando stroke can be played with a felt pick or a thumb and finger pick, but it sounds best without picks. Press the thumb and index finger together as you go up the strings. To make a smooth transition to the downstroke, slip the index finger forward just as you reach the highest strings. This produces a continuous harp-like sound. The fleshy part of the thumb touches the strings on the upstroke and the fleshy part of the index finger touches the strings on downstroke.

Begin by combining the up and down strokes in a continuous graceful motion over one or two measures of the music. This is a free-flowing type of stroke which is shown by this symbol: ⌢.

Notice that the next song uses the three principal chords in the key of D Major: D, G, and A7. Make a crescendo (play louder) in the middle of the strum, tapering off at the end. Your fingers may get sore at first, but soon they will form calluses, allowing you to play with ease, and make the Autoharp hum.

THE STREETS OF LAREDO

Chords Used: D, G, & A7

Cowboy Lament

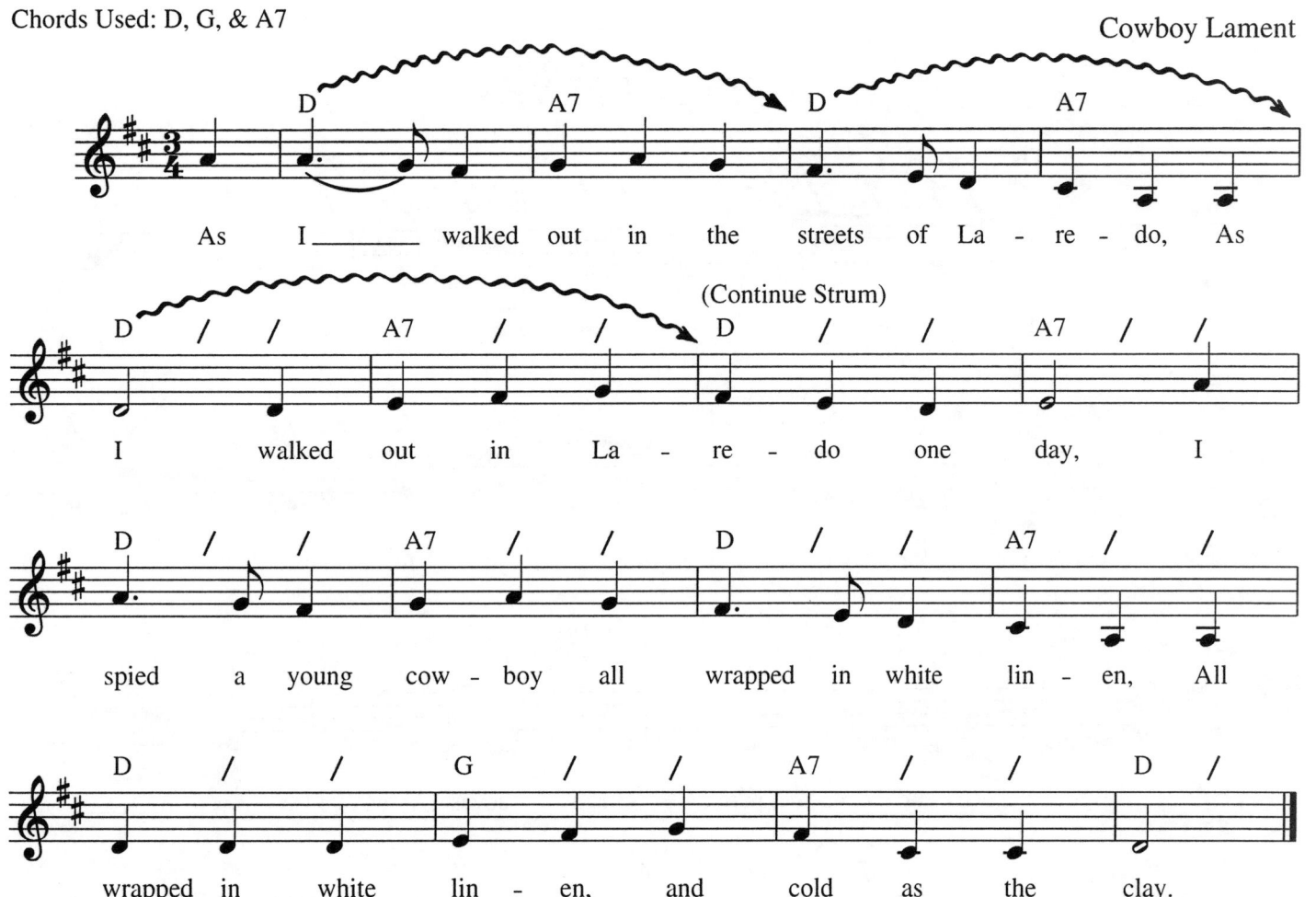

"Get six of my comrades to carry my coffin,
And six pretty maidens to sing a sad song,
Take me to the valley and lay the dirt over me
For I'm a young cowboy who played the game wrong."

"Go fetch me a cup, just a cup of cool water,
To cool my parched lips," the cowboy then said.
Before I returned, his spirit had left him
And gone to his Maker, the cowboy was dead.

For those whose fingers are still tender, play the second verse using the fingernail of the index finger on the upstroke and the fingernail of the thumb on the downstroke. The fingers are still pressed together, but the index finger, instead of the thumb, leads the way. You'll note that the sound is not as mellow, but it's more comfortable for beginners!

On the next song, combine an upstroke in the lower octave with two arpeggiando strokes in the two higher octaves. A thumb pick can be used, or the arpeggiando strokes can be done with the fingernail of the index finger.

This is the slow 6/8 rhythm mentioned on p.20. You will count all six beats, playing six strokes to the measure. Be sure to watch for the chord changes when they occur in the middle of the strum pattern.

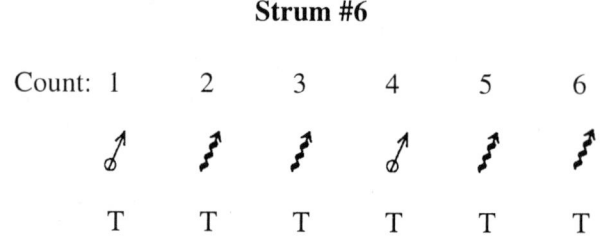

Strum #6

Count: 1 2 3 4 5 6
T T T T T T

Chords Used: Dm, A7, C, F, & B♭

GREENSLEEVES

Old English Ballad

Dm C B♭
A - las my love ___ you do me wrong ___ to cast me off ___ dis -
A7 (Continue Strum) Dm C
cour - teous - ly, for I have loved ___ you for so long ___ de -
Chorus:
B♭ A7 Dm F C
light - ing in ___ your com - pany. Green - sleeves ___ was all my joy. ___
Dm A7 F
Green - sleeves ___ was my de - light. Green - sleeves was my
C Dm A7 Dm
heart of gold ___ 'twas all for my la - dy ___ Green - sleeves.

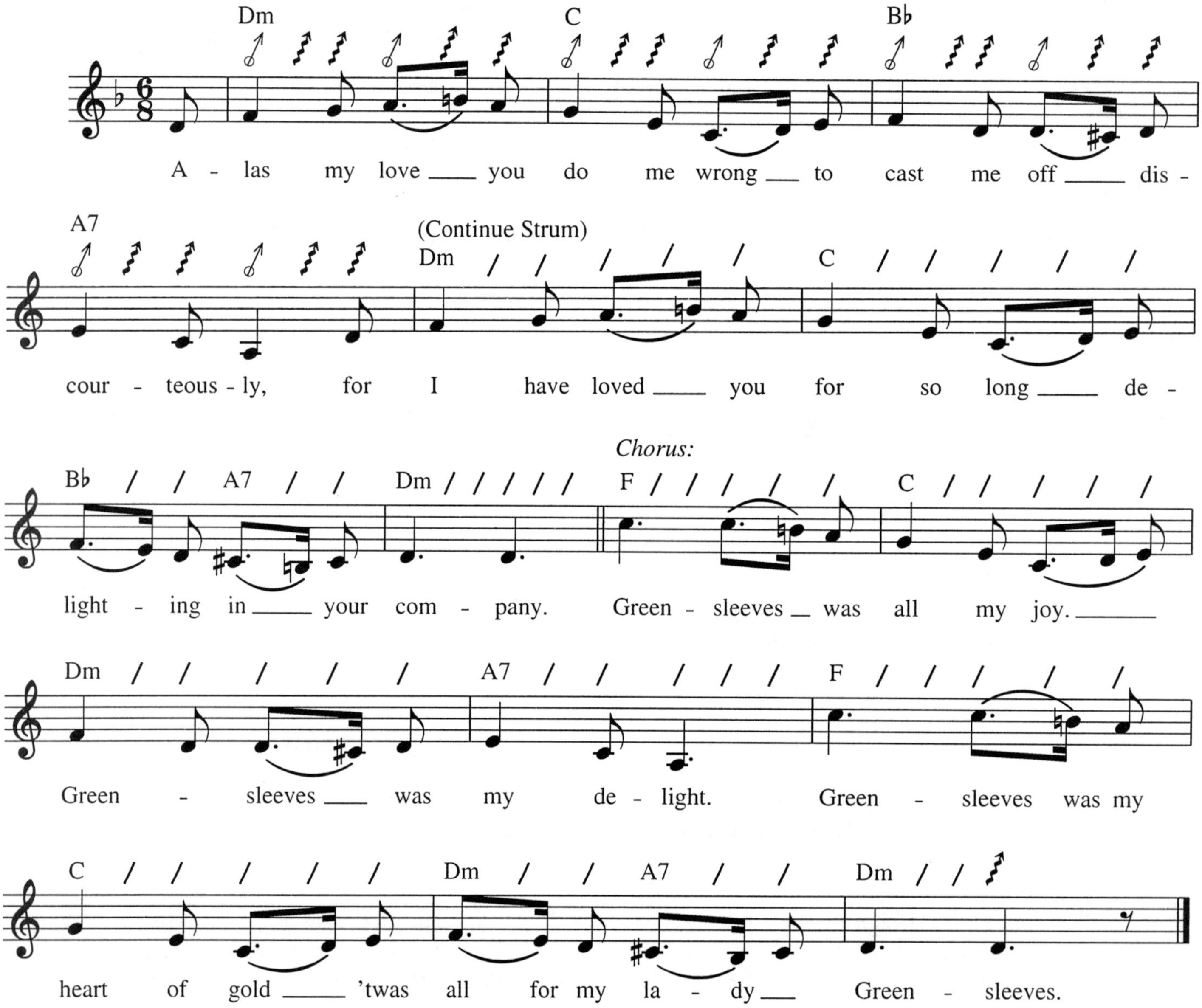

2. I have been ready at your hand
to grant whatever you would crave;
I have both wagered life and land
Your love and good–will for to have. *(Chorus)*

HOLDING THE AUTOHARP APPALACHIAN STYLE

Figure 16 shows how to hold the Autoharp in your arms Appalachian style, and figures 17 and 18 show you how to fit and wear a shoulder strap. You'll find that holding the instrument in this position frees your strumming arm for faster, more accurate playing and eliminates the "crossing over" necessary to get a good tone when the Autoharp is on your lap or a table.

You will have to adjust your fingering in this position. Choose the arrangement that most suits you.

Figure 16
Without Strap

Figure 17
With Strap

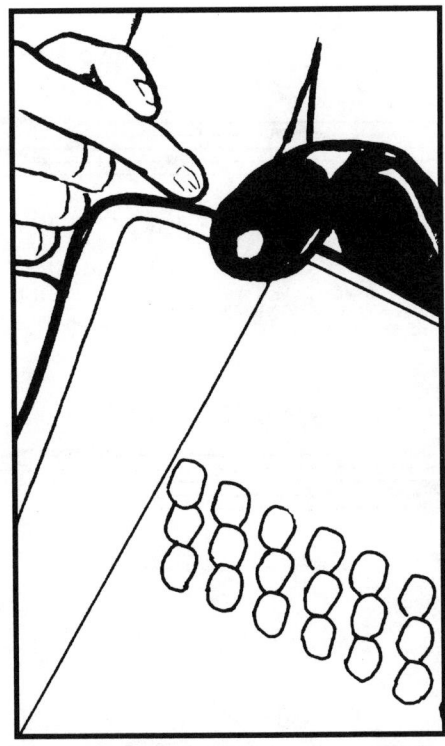

Figure 18
Strap Fitting

This next song lends itself to rapid arpeggiando upstrokes over the middle and higher octaves alternating with thumb upstrokes in the lower octave. It is arranged in fast 4/4 time. Count "1 and 2 and 3 and 4 and," using a short stroke in the lower octave on each beat followed by a longer arpeggiando stroke on the "and." The pattern looks like this:

Strum #7

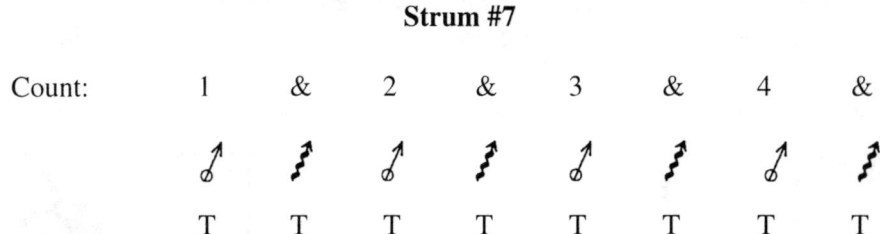

To make the pattern more interesting, try alternating the upstrokes in the lower octave, hitting the strings slightly higher on beats 2 and 4, but still remaining in the lower octave. Stroking eight times, rather than four, in each measure gives this song its joyous, upbeat mood.

You'll notice that the tune is arranged for the three principal chords in the key of G: G, C, & D7. The extra chords—A7, G7 and D—are not absolutely necessary, but are added for extra richness.

I'VE GOT PEACE LIKE A RIVER

Chords Used: G, C, D7, A7, G7, & D

Gospel Song

1. I've got peace like a riv-er, I've got peace like a riv-er, I've got peace like a riv-er in my soul; I've got peace like a riv-er, I've got peace like a riv-er, I've got peace like a riv-er in my soul.
2. I've got joy like a foun-tain, I've got joy like a foun-tain, I've got joy like a foun-tain in my soul, etc.
3. I've got love like an o-cean, I've got love like an o-cean, I've got love like an o-cean in my soul, etc.

THE CHURCH LICK

The arpeggiando stroke used in the previous song can also be played with a loose fist as shown in figure 19. Notice that the hand is relaxed as the fingernails brush across the strings. No picks are worn on the fingers, only a thumb pick on the thumb. The entire hand lifts off after the initial thumb stroke and the fingers come down on the strings with a fast, glancing stroke. Play the previous strum pattern using the loose fist (LF) instead of the thumb on the arpeggiando strokes.

Next, combine a fast upstroke arpeggiando with a fast downstroke arpeggiando (fig. 20), brushing the ends of your fingernails over strings in both the middle and the higher octaves as you did in the upstroke. There will be a spontaneous fanning out of the entire hand just before the downstroke arpeggiando is performed. The strum symbol looks like this:

Figure 19
An upstroke with the loose fist.

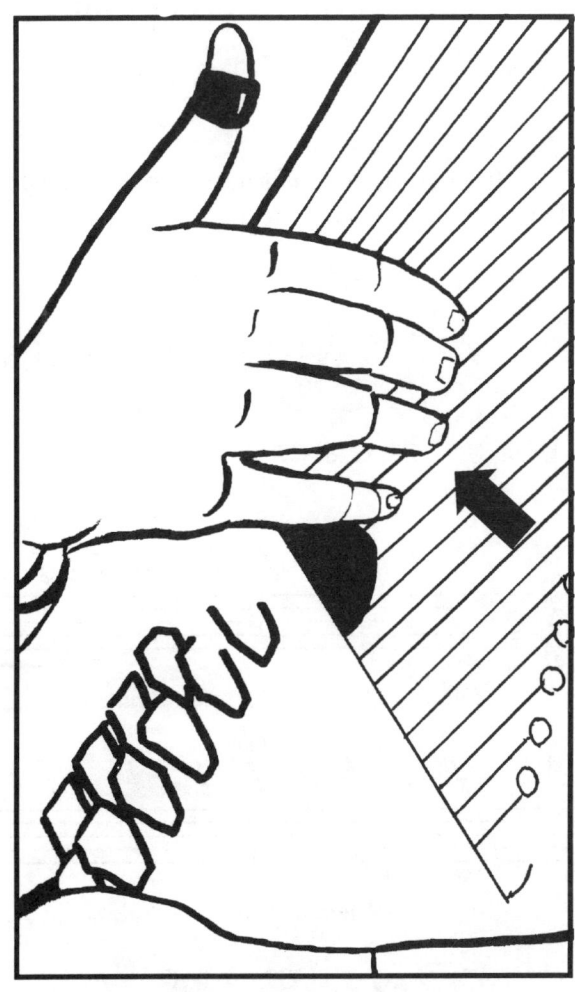

Figure 20
A downstroke with the loose fist.

This rapid up and down arpeggiando, combined with an upstroke with the thumb in the lower octave, is called the **Church Lick,** an adaptation of a guitar style made famous by Woody Guthrie. You've already become acquainted with up and down strokes in strum #5, p.30. In this next strum, however, you will have an up-down stroke pattern on "2 and" as well as "4 and."

Strum #8

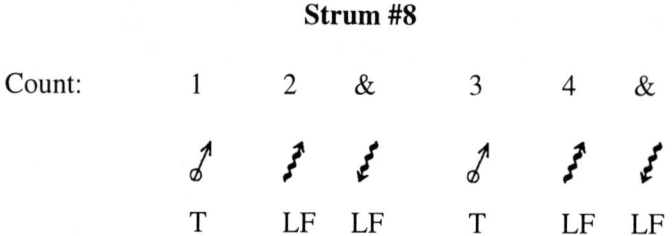

Count:	1	2	&	3	4	&
	T	LF	LF	T	LF	LF

As you practice this strum pattern, count and say:

one	two-and	three	four-and
thumb	loose-fist	thumb	loose-fist
up	up-down	up	up-down

Notice that the next song begins on the second beat of the strum. This is called the pick up and is counted "two-and, three, four-and, one," etc. Begin with the arpeggiando up-down pattern, and then move into the full 4/4 strum.

WHEN THE SAINTS GO MARCHING IN

Chords Used: C, F, G7, G, & C7

Black Traditional

Now move to the key of G and play another popular old tune which lends itself to the church Lick.

DOWN BY THE RIVERSIDE
(Ain't Gonna Study War No More)

Chords Used: G, C, D7, & G7

Spiritual

2. I'm gonna join hands with everyone, Down by the Riverside, etc.
3. I'm gonna put on my long white robe, Down by the Riverside, etc.
4. Gonna meet my Lord Je-sus, Down by the Riverside, etc.
5. Gonna lay down my sword and shield, Down by the Riverside, etc.

APPALACHIAN STRUMS

These next seven patterns are back-up strums used in bluegrass, country, and folk music. They form the basis for the traditional Appalachian Mountain Autoharp sound. Practice each one slowly, for accuracy, before building up speed.

THUMB LICK

This strum uses only the thumb. Play a short, accented upstroke in the lower octave followed by a fast up-down stroke in the middle octave (fig. 21). You may want to keep the thumb on the strings in the beginning, so that the middle octave up-down strokes become a continuation of the initial lower octave stroke. Later on, as you play faster, the thumb will automatically lift off just before the stroke in the middle octave begins.

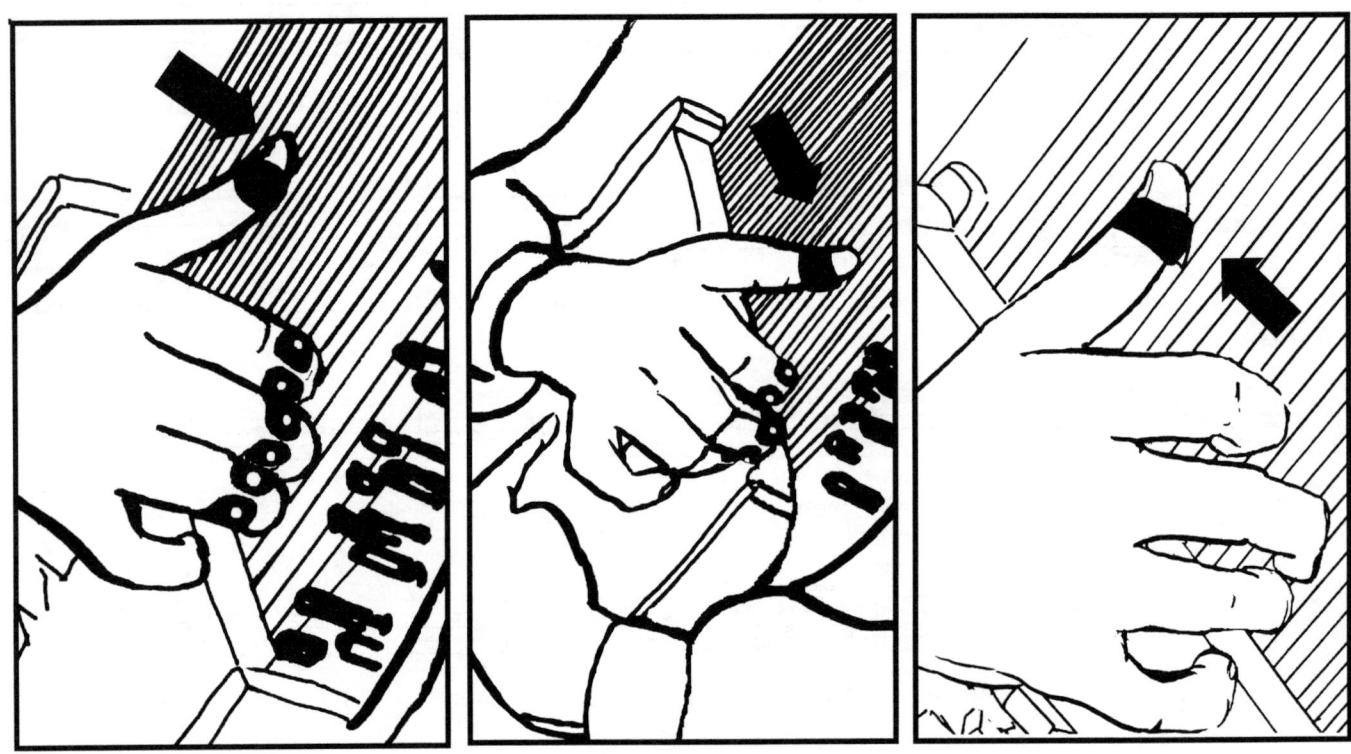

Figure 21
Thumb Lick

Strum #9

Count:	1	&	uh	2	&	uh
	T	T	T	T	T	T

Notice that each "& uh" pattern equals one single beat (the "1" or the "2"). Clap and count accordingly:

one	and-uh	two	and-uh
lower	mid-dle	lower	mid-dle
up	up-down	up	up-down

42

This rhythm sounds the same as Strum #8, but instead of counting "one, two-and, three, four-and" you will count "one, and-uh, two, and-uh." The difference is merely technical. Strum #8 is in 4/4 time; Strum #9 is in 2/4 time.

CAMPTOWN RACES

Chords Used: D, G, A7, & D7

Stephen Foster

The longtail filly and the big black horse Doo – Dah! Doo – Dah!
The fly the track and they both cut a cross Oh! Doo – Dah day.
The blind horse stuck in a big mud hole Doo – Dah! Doo – Dah!
He can't touch bottom with a ten foot pole Oh! Doo – Dah! Doo – Dah!
Chorus:

SCRATCH STYLE

Scratch style sounds very much like the thumb lick. The index finger, however, is executing the delicate up-down scratch in the middle octave instead of the thumb (fig. 22). This has come to be known as the "Carter Lick" after the famous Carter family. Mother Maybelle was known for this type of picking.

You will still use a rotating wrist, as in all Appalachian styles. Do not run the index finger straight up the strings, but gently brush them with the fingernail in a **glancing, slightly diagonal fashion.** This can be done with or without a finger pick.

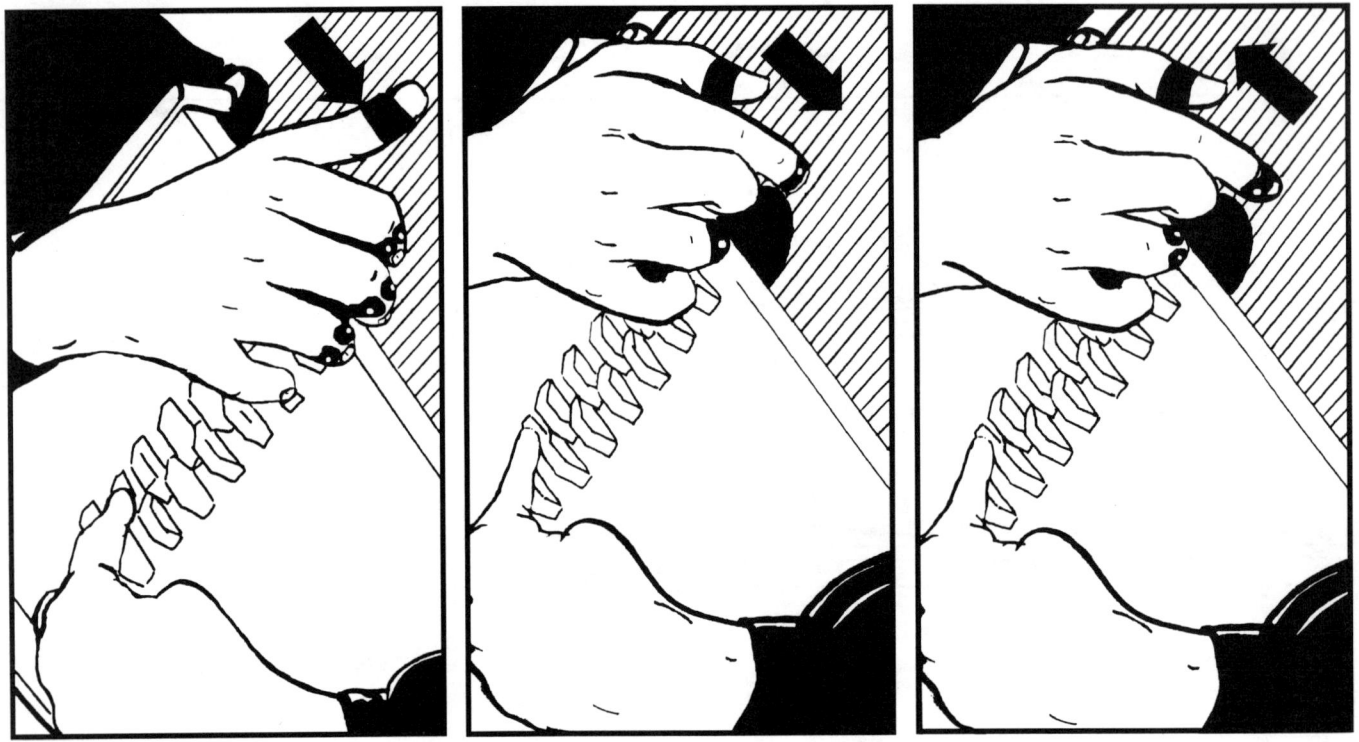

Figure 22
Scratch Style

Strum #10

Count:	1	2	&	3	4	&
	♩	♪	♪	♩	♪	♪
	T	i*	i	T	i	i

i = a stroke with the index finger

This strum is in 4/4 time, so will be counted like this:

one	two - and	three	four - and
lower	mid - dle	lower	mid - dle
Thumb	in - dex	Thumb	in - dex

LITTLE BROWN JUG

Chords Used: C, F, G7, & C7

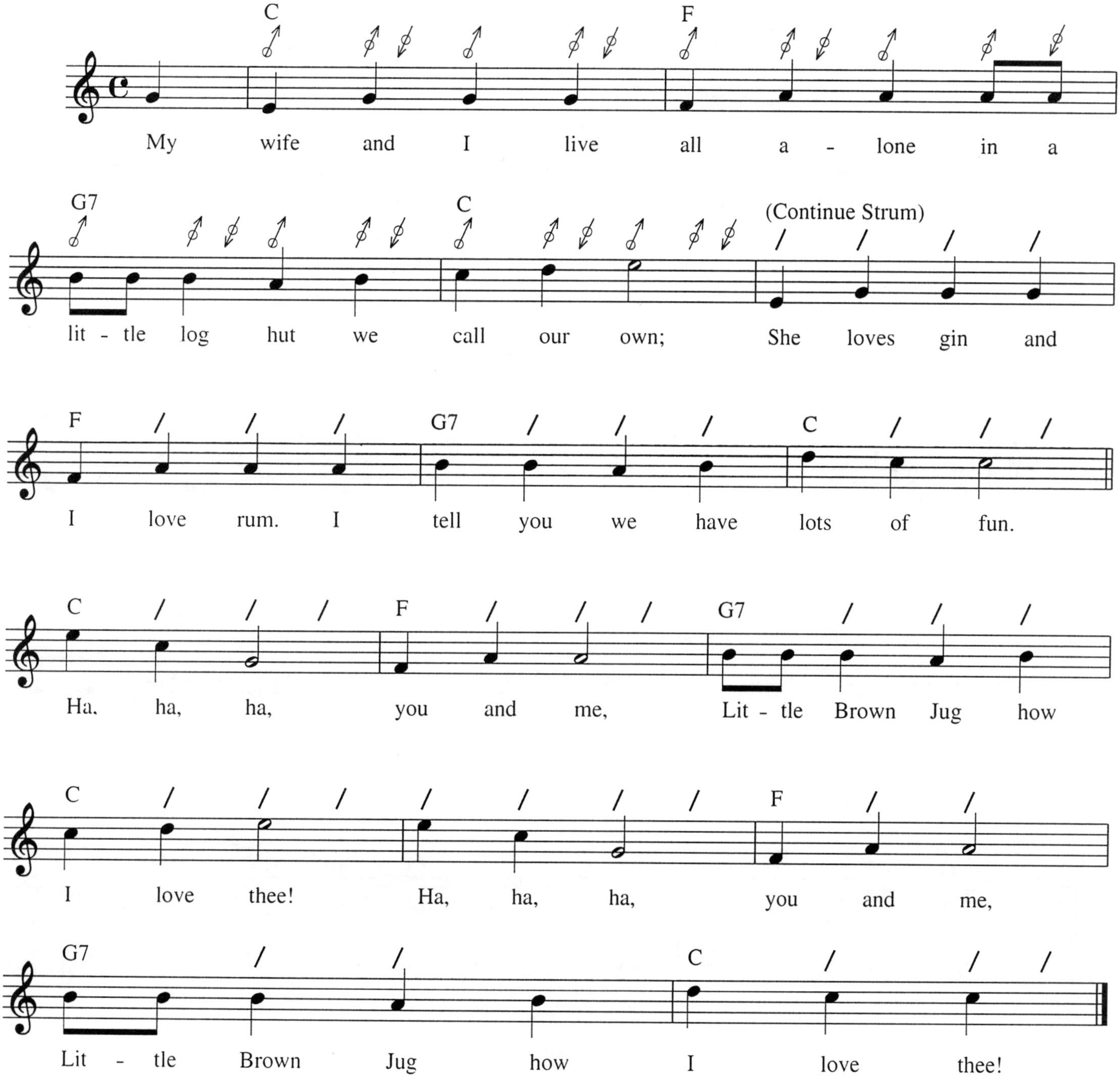

My wife and I live all a-lone in a lit-tle log hut we call our own; She loves gin and I love rum. I tell you we have lots of fun. Ha, ha, ha, you and me, Lit-tle Brown Jug how I love thee! Ha, ha, ha, you and me, Lit-tle Brown Jug how I love thee!

Scratch style can also be played in 3/4 time.

Strum #11

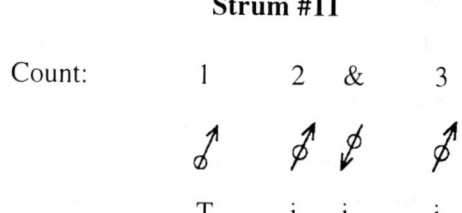

Notice that Strum #11 has only one light upstroke in the middle octave on count "3." Practice counting out loud:

one	two - and	three
lower	mid - dle	middle
Thumb	in - dex	index

After you've learned the pattern this way, you can play it a second time, adding a downstroke on the 3rd beat and counting "1, 2&, 3&." Practice the strum both ways and play it on this old pioneer song.

SWEET BETSY FROM PIKE

Chords Used: C, F, G7, G, & Am

Traditional

Oh — don't you re-mem-ber Sweet Bet-sy From Pike Who

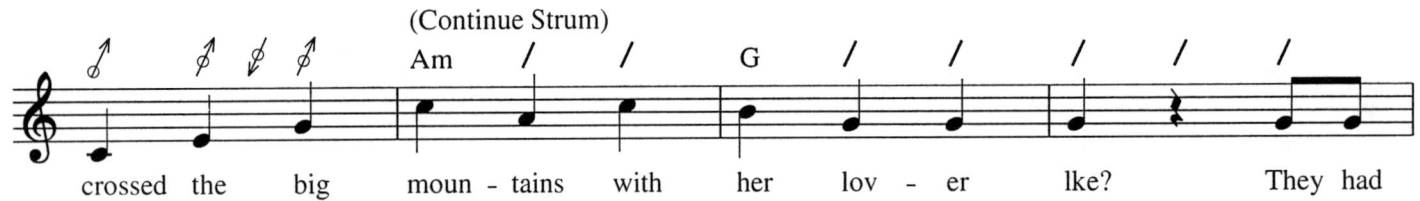

crossed the big moun-tains with her lov-er Ike? They had

two yoke of cat-tle And a large yel-ler dog. And a

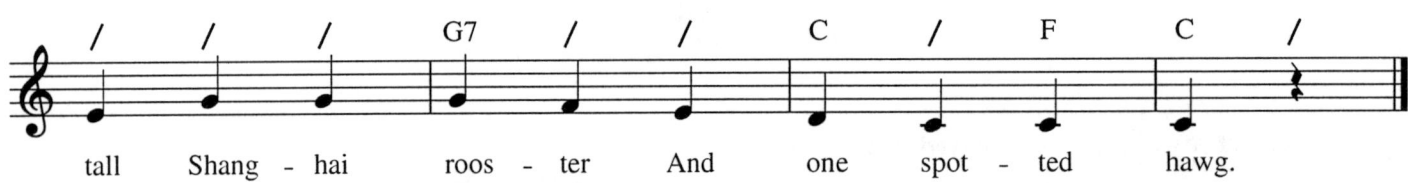

tall Shang-hai roos-ter And one spot-ted hawg.

2. One evening quite early they camped on the Platt
  "Twas near by the road on a green shady flat;
  Where Betsy, quite tired, lay down to repose,
  While with wonder Ike gazed on his Pike County Rose.

3. The Injuns came down in a wild yelling horde
  And Betsy got scared they would scalp her adored
  So behind the front wagon wheel Betsy did crawl
  And fought off the Injuns with musket and ball.

4. They passed the Sierras through mountains of snow
  'Till old California was sighted below
  Sweet Betsy she hollered and Ike gave a cheer
  Sayin', "Betsy, my darling, I'm a made millionaire."

DOUBLE FINGER SCRATCH

To play a double finger scratch, start with a thumb upstroke in the lower octave followed by a fast up-down pattern in the middle octave, this time played with the index and middle fingers held together (fig. 23). It will give you more volume as well as a firmer control over the stroke. You do not need to wear finger picks, since the fingernails of both fingers will brush the strings simultaneously.

Figure 23
Double Finger Scratch

This next 4/4 strum is counted and played like Strum #10, p. 44, only a Double Finger Scratch is used in the middle octave instead of the index finger. Practice repeating your octave designations as you did for Strum #10, substituting DF for index finger.

Strum #12

Count:	1	2	&	3	4	&
	♪	♪	♪	♪	♪	♪
	T	DF*	DF	T	DF	DF

DF = a scratch stroke played with the index and middle fingers together

SHE WORE A YELLOW RIBBON

Chords Used: D, & A7

American College Song

A-round her hair, She wore a yel-low rib-bon; She wore it in the spring-time and in the month of May, And if you asked her why the heck she wore it, She wore it for her sol-dier boy who's far, far a-way. Far a-

Chorus

way, _____ far a-way _____ She wore it for her sol-dier boy who's far, far-a-way._____

But, in her heart, she has a secret passion
She has it in the springtime, and in the month of May;
And if you asked her who is now her passion,
She has it for a college man who's not so far away.   *(Chorus)*

* a single arpeggiande stroke can be used to end the song.

Now use the Double Finger Scratch on an old 3/4 tune. Instead of a single upstroke with the index finger in the middle octave on the count of "3," as in Strum #11, p.45, play two strokes (up-down) with the index and middle finger together on the count of "3 &" like this:

Strum #13

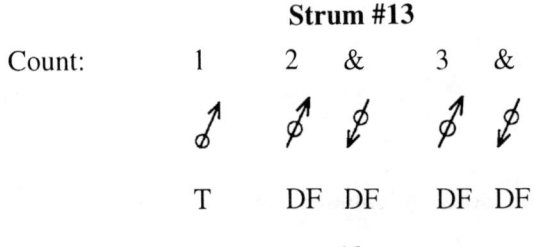

48

THE SIDEWALKS OF NEW YORK
(East Side, West Side)

Chords Used: F, B♭, C7 F7, D7, G7, & C

Words & Music by
C. B. Lawlor & J. W. Blake

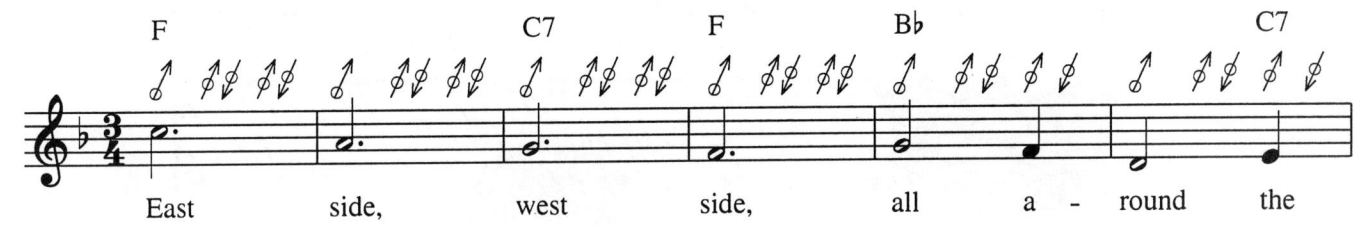

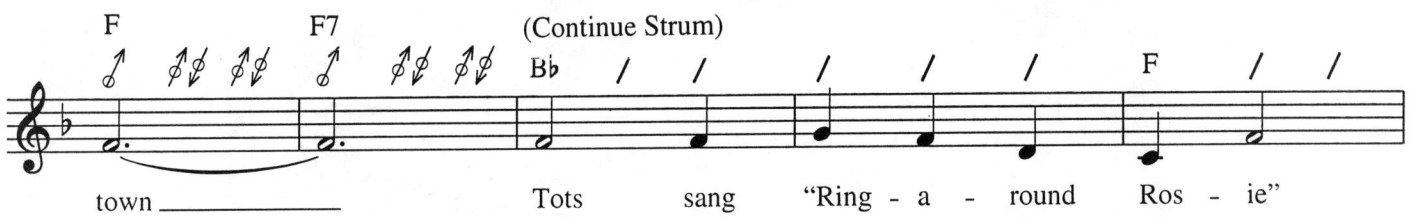

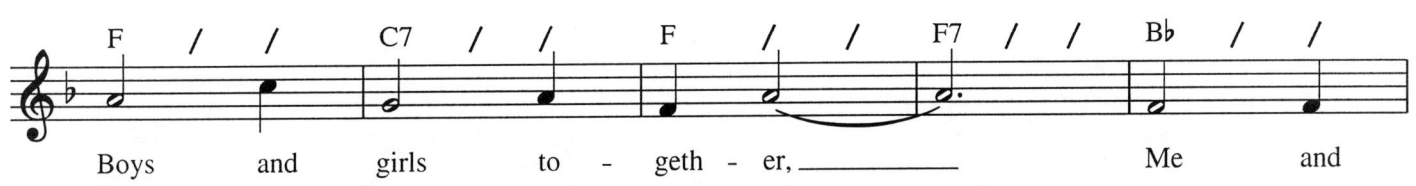

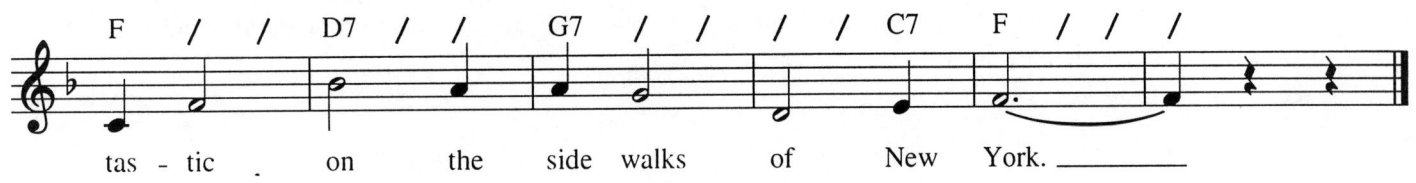

INTRODUCING THE MIDDLE FINGER

This next strum is counted the same as Strum #10, p.44, but the middle finger plays the fast downstroke on the count of "&" in the higher octave (Fig. 24), instead of the index finger playing it in the middle octave.

Figure 24
Downstroke with the middle finger

Strum #14

Count:	1	2	&	3	4	&
	T	i	m*	T	i	m

m = a stroke with the middle finger

To execute this pattern, accent the first thumb stroke, then barely touch two or three strings with the index and middle fingers in the middle and higher octaves respectively. This is a delicate strum similar to the scratch style, but the downstroke in the higher octave gives the music that "twangy" sound so familiar to country pickers.

This is a real tongue-twister! Practice aloud, until you have internalized the octave designations and automatically know which fingers play in each octave.

one	two - and	three	four - and
lower	middle - higher	lower	middle - higher
thumb	index - middle	thumb	index - middle

THE CRAWDAD SONG

Chords Used: D, G, A7, G7, & D7

Country Folk

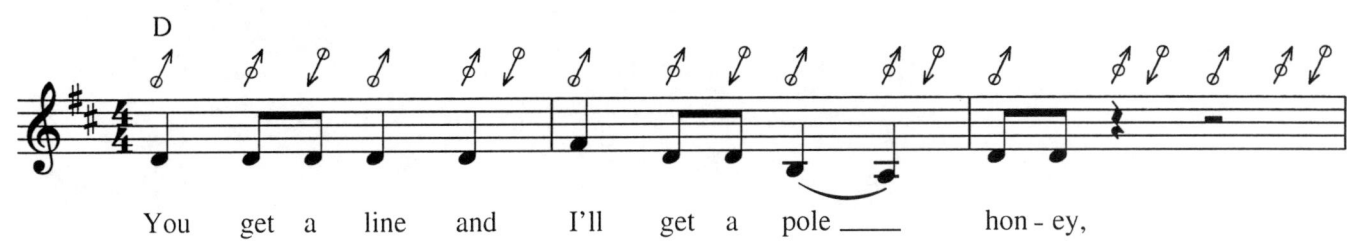
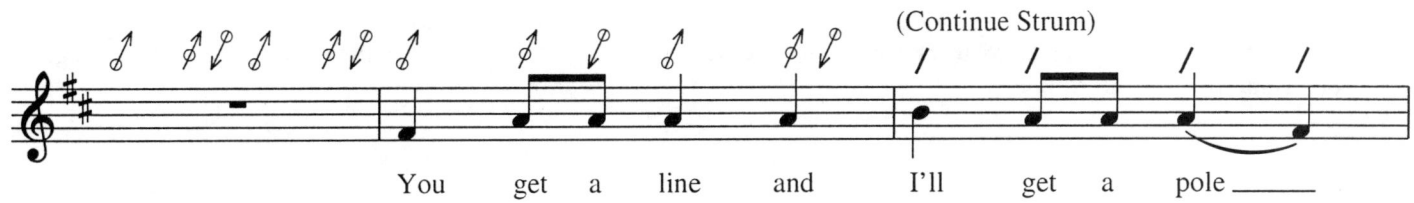
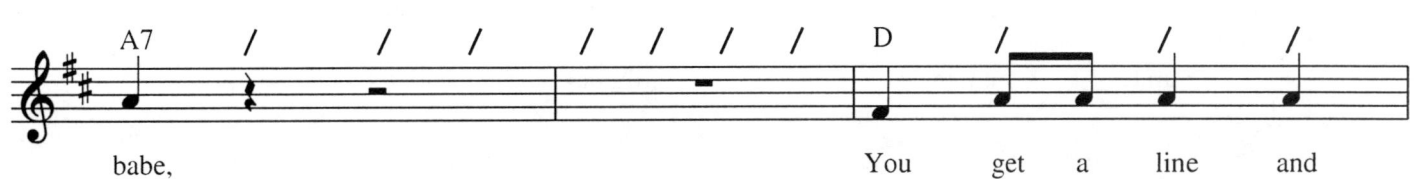
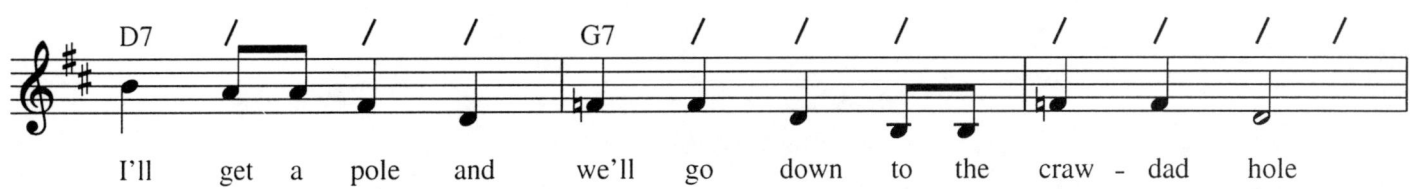
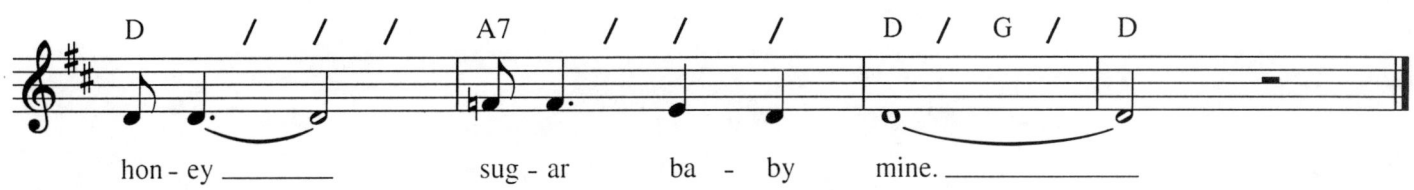

What you gonna do when the lake runs dry, honey?
What you gonna do when the lake runs dry, Babe?
What you gonna do when the lake runs dry,
Sit on the banks and watch the crawdads die?
Honey, Sugar baby mine.

Another strum uses an accented upstrokes with the thumb in the lower octave followed by two delicate downstrokes with middle and index fingers in the higher and middle octaves respectively. This time the middle finger plays before the index finger.

Instead of up, up-down as in Strum #14, the pattern is up, down-down. The count is the same.

Strum #15

Count:	1	2	&	3	4	&
	↑	↓	↓	↑	↓	↓
	T	m	i	T	m	i

This is another tongue-twister. Be sure not to confuse the octave designations in the second line with the finger designations in the third line.

one	two	-	and	three	four	-	and
lower	higher	-	middle	lower	higher	-	middle
thumb	middle	-	index	thumb	middle	-	index

If you get this pattern going fast on the next song, it sounds almost like horses galloping. No wonder it's a favorite of the young people.

SHE'LL BE COMIN' ROUND THE MOUNTAIN
(When She Comes)

Chorus Used: G, C, D7, & G7

Traditional

2. She'll be drivin' six white horses when she comes...

3. And we'll all go out to met her when she comes...

4. And we'll kill the old red rooster when she comes...

5. And we'll all have chicken and dumplings when she comes...

ARPEGGIO STRUMS

Arpeggio strums on the Autoharp simulate the sound of a traditional guitar accompaniment, where the fingers pluck consecutive single notes in a gentle flowing manner. To obtain this effect, use the thumb, index, and middle fingers—one after the other in the order of the particular strum pattern—and pluck as few strings as possible in each octave. Move up and down the 36 strings, trying to sound a different string on each stroke. Think of yourself as playing a "broken chord" rather than a specific stroke in each octave. If your touch is delicate, you will sound only one or two strings at a time, thus giving the feeling of single string picking.

As the tempo (speed) increases you'll notice that you're plucking in a different area within the designated octave on each successive stroke. It is important that you vary the strokes, since this is a free-flowing, relaxed style. **The stroke symbols merely denote the direction in which the fingers move.** For clarity and uniformity of sound, use picks on your thumb and fingers.

Strum #16

Count:	1	&	2	&	3	&
	↑	↓	↓	↓	↑	↓
	T	i	m	i	T	i

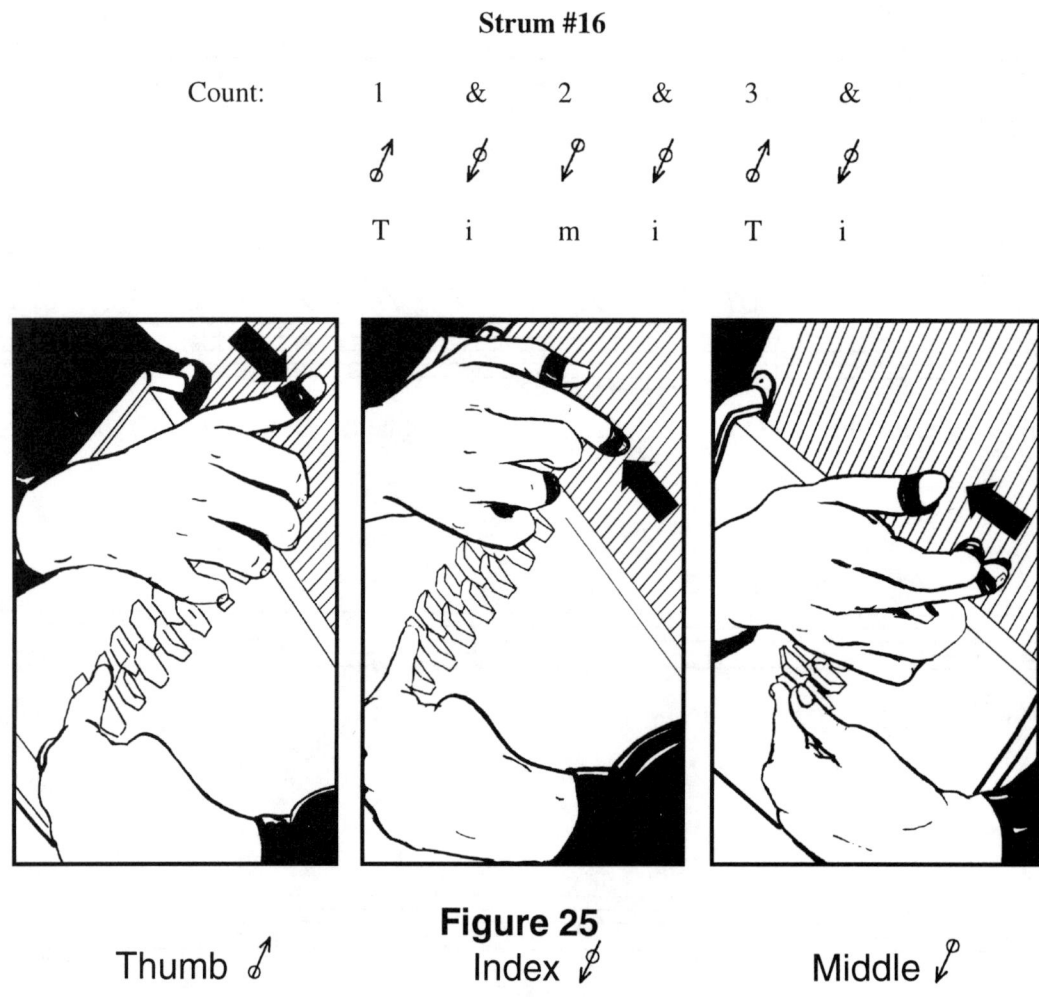

Figure 25

Thumb ↑   Index ↓   Middle ↓

Look at Figure 25 and count this 3/4 pattern out loud several times. Rotate your wrist as you practice moving smoothly from one finger to the other, and from one octave to the other.

one	-	and	two	-	and	three	-	and
lower	-	middle	higher	-	middle	lower	-	middle
thumb	-	index	middle	-	index	thumb	-	index

SCARBOROUGH FAIR

Chords Used: Am, G, C, D, & F

English folk song

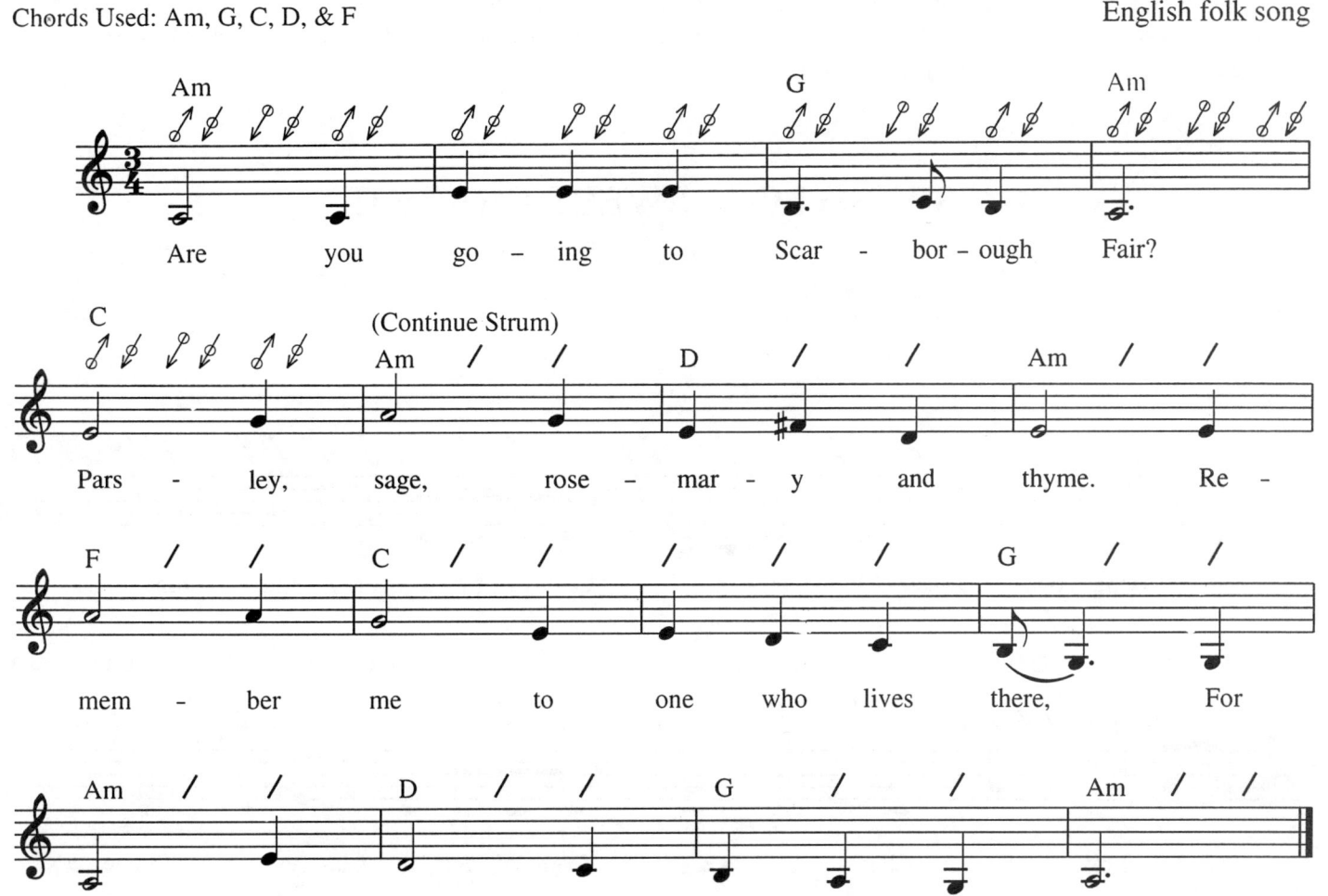

Next, let's try a 4/4 arpeggio strum.

Strum #17

Count this the same as the previous strum, adding the middle and index fingers on the count of "4 &."

This next old spiritual will be a challenge to most beginners, because it changes frequently in the middle of the strum pattern. Be sure to keep the strum going during these changes.

Some of the changes, however, as in measures seven and fifteen, are not necessary for the harmony, but merely add richness to the accompaniment. I've put the optional chords in parentheses. Try playing the song both ways and see if you don't prefer the more frequent changes. Be sure to locate all chords, decide what fingering you'll use, and practice the changes before playing the song.

SWING LOW, SWEET CHARIOT

Chords Used: C, F, G7, C7, D7, Am, & G   Spiritual

* = Optional Chord

TRAVIS PICKING

This next style of playing also uses the thumb, index, and middle fingers, but in an alternating, not a consecutive pattern. The thumb alternates with the index and middle fingers of the right hand in a delicate pattern, a kind of perpetual motion. The fingers do not wiggle, but gently brush the strings, and the wrist rotates with each stroke. This is the style that guitar players use most frequently when they play Autoharp back-up or rhythmic fillers during melody picking. It derives its name from the guitar style make popular by Merle Travis.

Notice that the thumb always plays an **upstroke on the beat** and the index and middle fingers alternate with a **downstroke off the beat** (on the count of "&"). When you get the strum up to tempo, the strokes will automatically be short. In fact, they will sound like individual strings being picked out of the dampened chord. Be sure to aim for a different section of each octave on each successive stroke. This will make your accompaniment more interesting and fun to play.

As in arpeggio style, the arrows in the pattern merely indicate the direction of the picking motion.

Strum #18

Count:	1		2	&	3	&
	♩		♩	♪	♪	♪
	T		T	i	T	m

Count, and repeat the octave designations and fingering as you practice:

one	two - and	three - and
lower	lower - middle	middle - higher
thumb	thumb - index	thumb - middle

Notice how your fingers move up the strings, playing in a slightly different area of the octave, even when there are two strokes in the same octave (as in count 1 and 2). Always keep in mind that octaves on the Autoharp are not rigid areas, but general guidelines.

THE MORE WE GET TOGETHER

Chords Used: F & C7

Lively

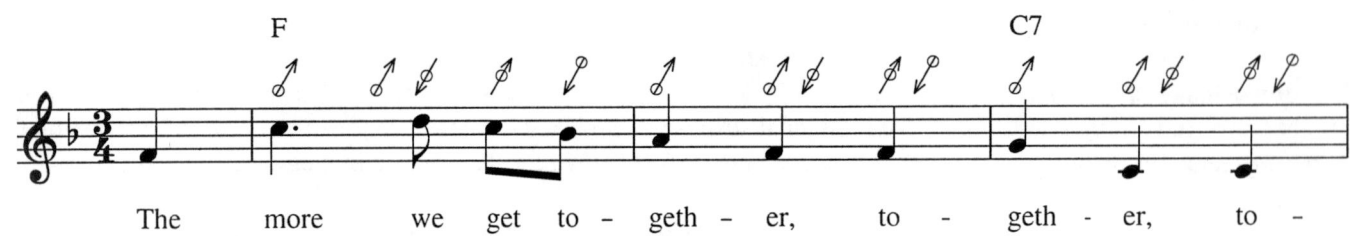
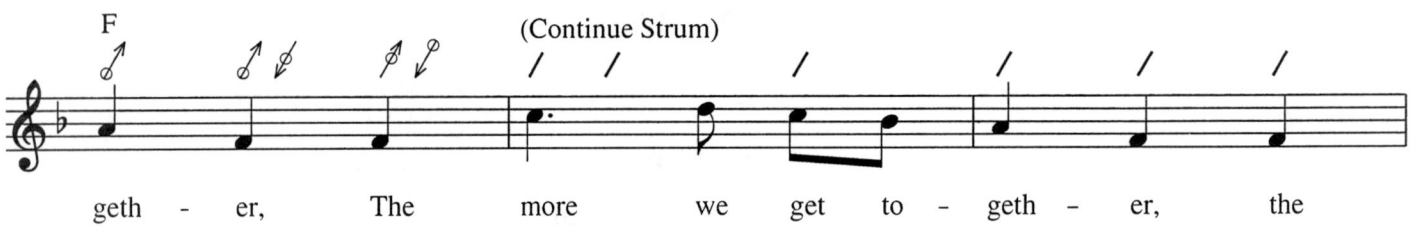
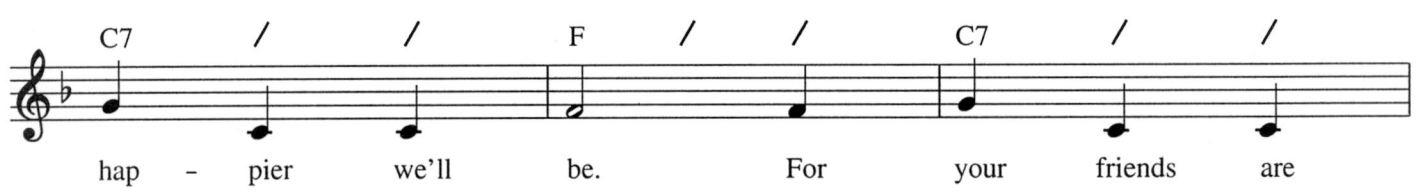
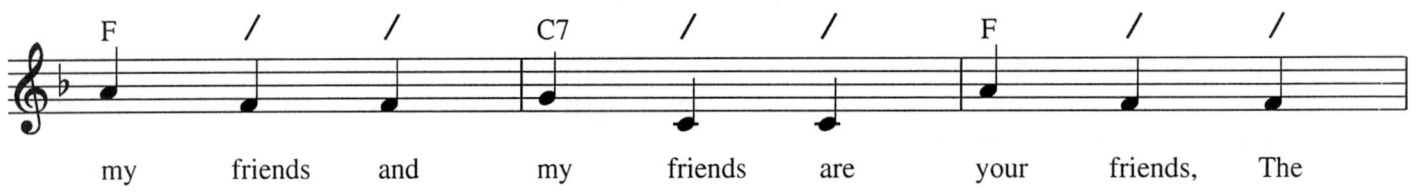
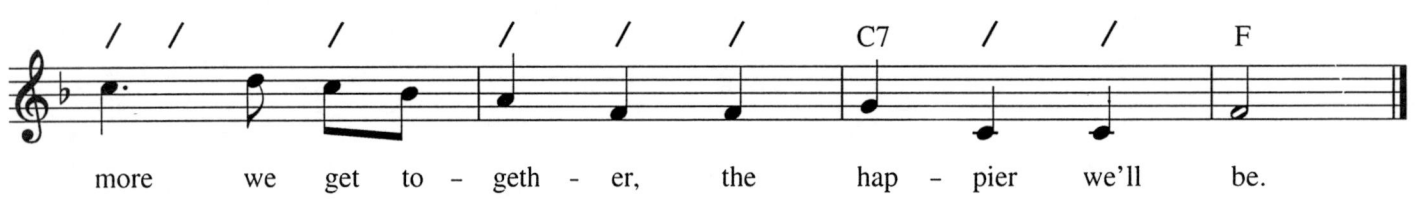

Now, let's try Travis picking in 4/4.

Strum #19

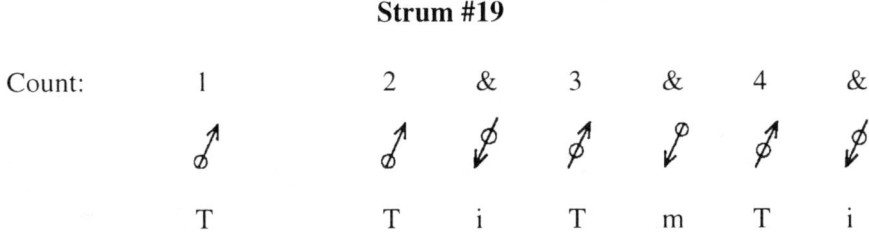

Practice this pattern the same as the previous strum, adding a thumb and index stroke on the count of "4 &."

MICHAEL, ROW THE BOAT ASHORE

Chords Used: C, F, & G7   Traditional

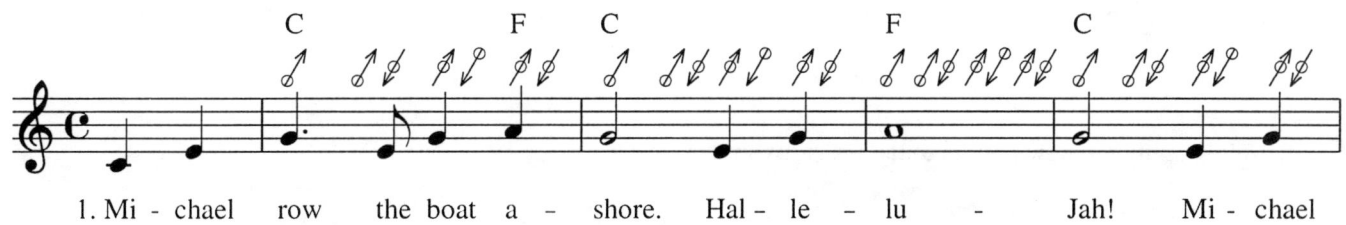

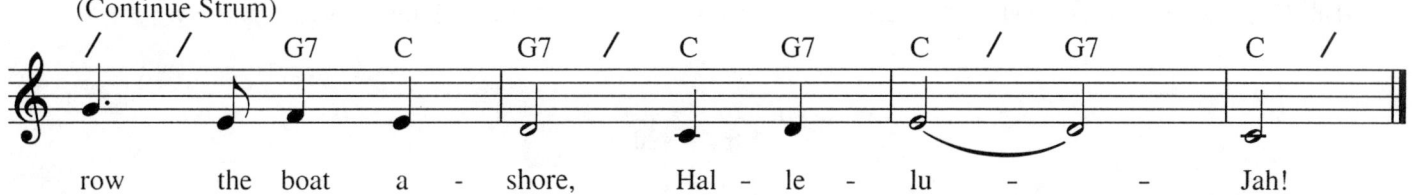

    2. Sister help me trim the sail,
       Hallelujah!
       Sister help me trim he sail,
       Hallelujah!

    3. Jordan river is chilly and cold,
       Hallelujah!
       Chills the body but not the soul.
       Hallelujah!

    4. Land of Canaan on the other side,
       Hallelujah!
       Land of Canaan on the other side,
       Hallelujah!

    5. We are bound for the promised land,
       Hallelujah!
       We are bound for the promised land,
       Hallelujah!

    6. I have heard the good news too
       Hallelujah!
       I have heard the good news too
       Hallelujah!

For variety, change Strum #19 slightly by adding an index stroke on the first offbeat, so that all the offbeats are now played. This will change the order of alternating strokes to look like this:

Strum #19a

Count:	1	&	2	&	3	&	4	&
	T	i	T	m	T	i	T	m
	>							

As before, the strum starts in the lower octave and moves smoothly up the strings to the higher octave and back down again, in a perfect loop. It will be counted:

one - and	two - and	three - and	four - and
lower - middle	middle - higher	middle - middle	lower - middle
thumb - index	thumb - middle	thumb - index	thumb - middle

Now apply the new pattern to the previous song.

The final Travis strum starts with a wide pinch executed by the thumb and middle finger plucking in the lower and the higher octaves respectively. The **pinch** (P) is followed by alternating index, thumb, and middle finger strokes.

Strum #20

Count:	1	&	2	&	3	&	4	&
	P							**
	(T-m)*	i	T	m	T	i	T	(rest)

* = a wide pinch using the thumb and middle finger
** = an eighth rest

You'll notice that this strum is counted the same as #19a, except that there is no stroke on the final half of the fourth beat. This short rest gives your hand a chance to open up and get ready for the initial pinch in the next measure. It will help you understand the sequence of the octaves and the changes in fingering if you count out loud as you practice:

one - and	two - and	three - and	four
pinch - middle	lower - higher	middle - middle	lower
(T-m) - index	thumb - middle	thumb - index	thumb

WHEN YOU AND I WERE YOUNG, MAGGIE

Chords Used: G, C, D7, G7, and A7

J. A. Butterfield

For further study of arpeggio and Travis strums, see *Mel Bay's Complete Book of Traditional & Country Autoharp Picking Styles* by Meg Peterson, 1986, and *The Complete Method for Autoharp or Chromaharp* by Meg Peterson, 1979; Mel Bay Publications, Pacific, MO, 63069.

MELODY PICKING

So far you've learned twenty strums that can be used to accompany solo singing, or as back-up with a group of instrumentalists, each of whom will take a turn playing the melody. In this section you'll learn to play melody on the Autoharp, so that you, too, can take your turn with the rest of the musicians.

Playing melody on the Autoharp is done by pressing down the designated chord and pinching gently with the thumb and index, or thumb and middle finger in the area of the melody note (string),

You are not plucking an open string, but merely pinching in the correct section of the depressed chord. You do not need to be precise, since two or more strings on either side of the melody string are automatically dampened. You can even miss the exact string and still sound the correct note.

In melody strumming you stroke up to the melody string, but **in melody picking**—which is by far the preferred method—**the index or middle finger plucks the melody string.** The function of the thumb is to add rhythm and harmony, and its position is optional: wider apart for more depth of sound, and closer together for faster picking.

Thumb and finger picks are not essential, but will give you a louder, brighter tone and will also protect your fingers. After you've developed calluses, you may wish the more gentle tone produced by playing without picks.

To understand the concept of melody playing on the Autoharp, press down the C chord and gently pinch in small intervals from the lower to the higher octaves and back again. You will hear seven or eight melody notes (strings) on that one chord alone. Now press the F chord and do the same. Then the G7 chord, and back to the C chord. Notice how many different melody strings are sounded on these three chords alone. You can play whole melodies by ear on one or two chords, or make them up as you go along. Just listen as you play and think of each sounded string as a melody note, not just a chord interval.

Now, press the C chord again, and try playing the familiar song "Taps" by starting on the 8th string or the 19th string, and going up when the melody goes up and down when it goes down. Pinch as in figures 26 and 27, making sure your fingers come together about two inches off the strings. **This is a delicate brush-like motion, not a grabbing or dragging together of the fingers.** The strings should be touched in such a way that the melody rings on every pinch.

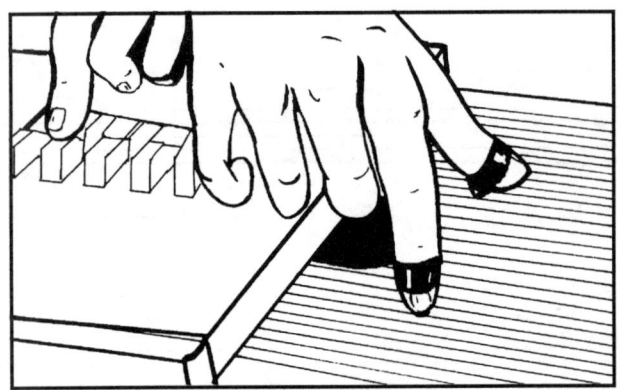

Figure 26
Hand ready to pinch

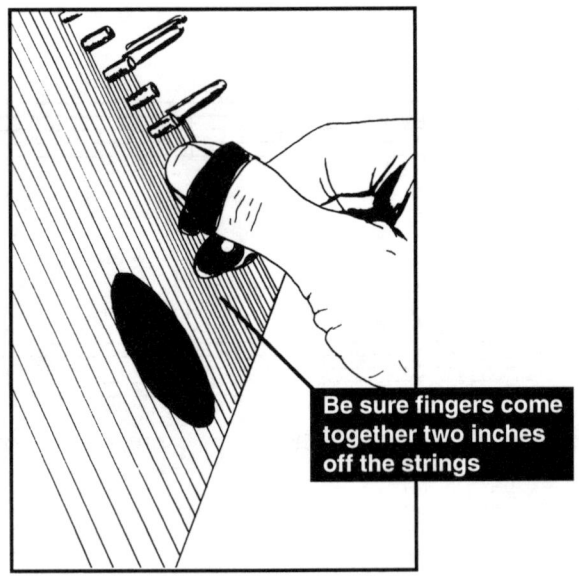

Figure 27
Completed pinch

Be sure fingers come together two inches off the strings

If, at first, you have trouble hearing the melody, you can learn it by looking at the written music, and locating the melody by string number. To help you do this, there is a musical scale label on most 15 chord Autoharps at the wide end under the strings (figure 28). The small white numbers printed in units of five will give you an indication of the specific area in which to pinch.

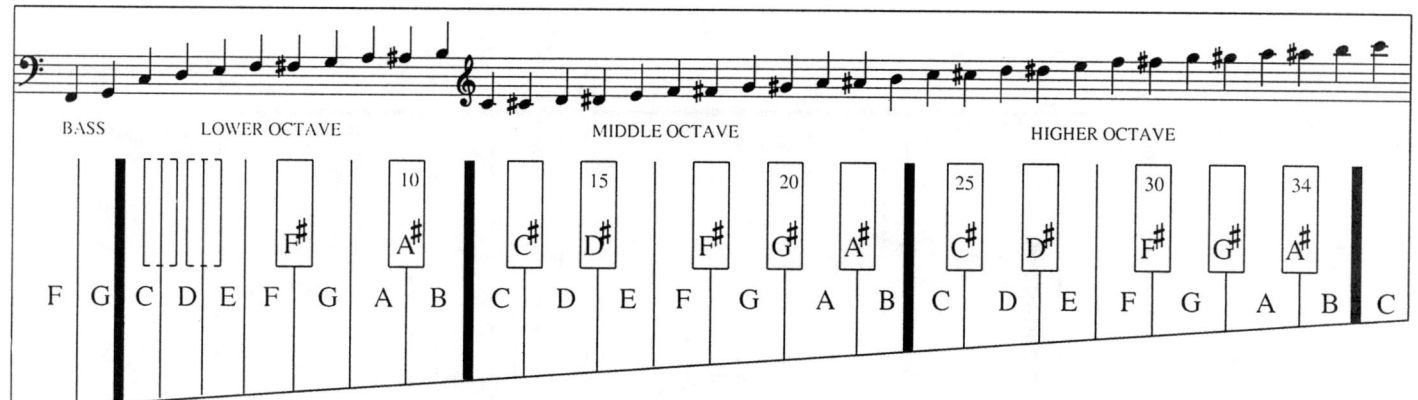

Figure 28

Scale Label

To further understand the following scoring system used to play melody, and to see graphically how the Autoharp strings relate to the musical staff, see figure 29.

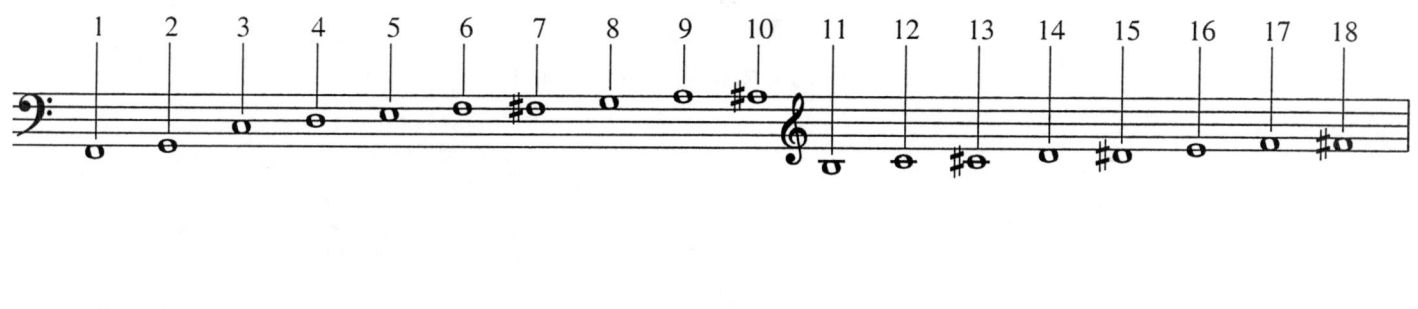

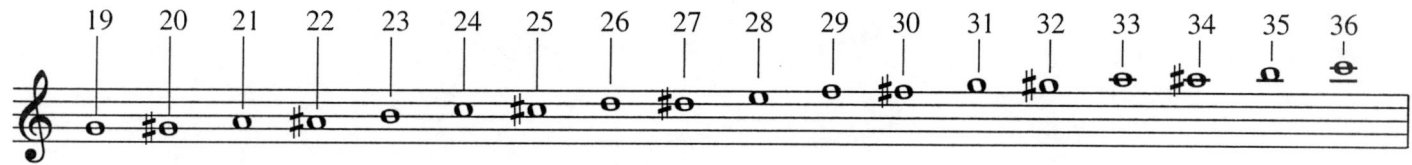

Figure 29

Numbered Autoharp strings as they appear on the musical staff

Even if you don't understand standard musical notation, this will help you see the pattern—the ups and downs—of the melody so you can figure out familiar and unfamiliar tunes by number. As you can see, each string on the Autoharp has been numbered from the lowest (1) to the highest (36), so that as the melody goes up in pitch, so do the numbers.

For those of you who have no scale label, it may be helpful to cut out the melody aid on p.94 and place it under the strings to the left of the chord bars, with the heavy line under the lowest string. Fasten it on one end with tape as in figure 30.

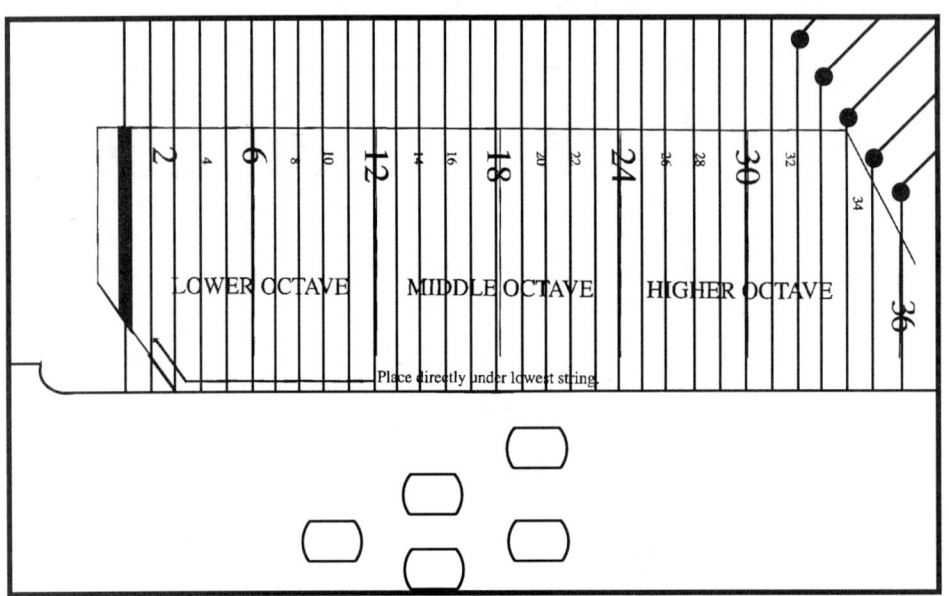

Figure 30
Melody Aid,
With Strings numbered in intervals

Now look at "Taps," which you have just played by ear, and see how the numbers help you find the melody strings more accurately. The chord appears above the string number and is not repeated between chord changes. In this case, the C chord is used throughout the piece.

TAPS

* / = repeat the preceding chord and melody note

Melody picking on the Autoharp requires more frequent chord changes than straight back-up accompanying. You may have noticed when you played "Michael, Row the Boat Ashore" (p.59), that the changes in the second line of music seemed to bring out the melody, even while you were playing an accompaniment strum. This was caused by an increase in the use of the V (G) or V7 (G7) chord of the key in which the song was written.

The next song, "Row, Row, Row Your Boat," can be played with two chords in simple strumming—the C chord throughout, changing to the G7 in the next to the last measure. When playing melody, however, you'll have to change back and forth from the C (I) to the G7 (V7) chord in nearly every measure in order to sound the correct melody string.

While you're getting acquainted with the location of the melody strings, you may want to hold the Autoharp on your lap. Soon, however, you'll find that holding it Appalachian style (fig. 7, p.8) will allow you more freedom of arm and finger movement as well as a more resonant tone.

ROW, ROW, ROW YOUR BOAT

Chords Used: C, F, & G7   Traditional

In this next old favorite, you can add a simple thumb stroke to keep the rhythm going. It will look like this ↗.

Notice that the entire tune is played with changes between the I (D) and the V7 (A7) chords.

CLEMENTINE

Chords Used: D, & A7

Traditional

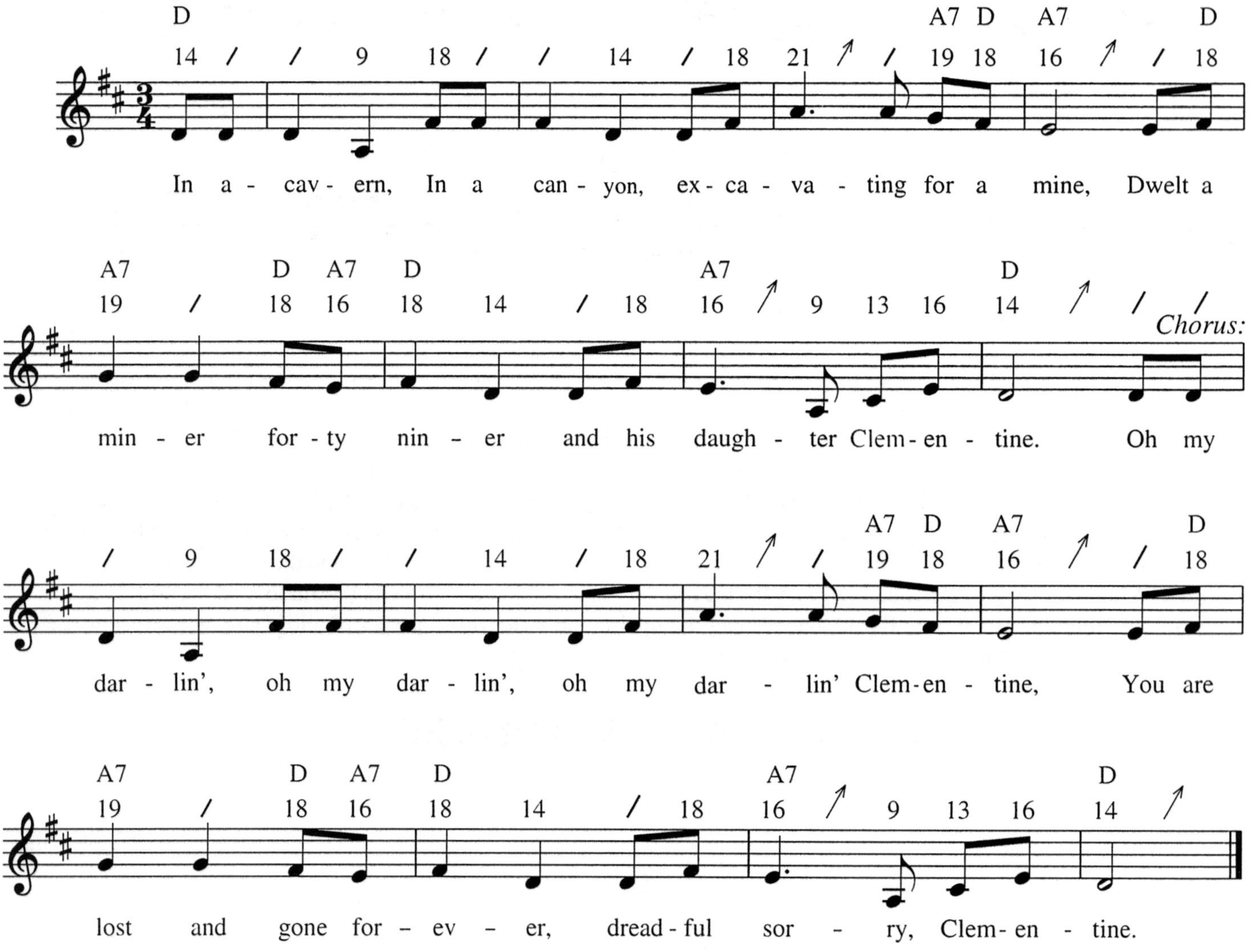
D A7 D A7 D
14 / / 9 18 / / 14 / 18 21 ↗ / 19 18 16 ↗ / 18
In a - cav - ern, In a can - yon, ex - ca - va - ting for a mine, Dwelt a
A7 D A7 D A7 D
19 / 18 16 18 14 / 18 16 ↗ 9 13 16 14 ↗ / /
Chorus:
min - er for - ty nin - er and his daugh - ter Clem - en - tine. Oh my
A7 D A7 D
/ 9 18 / / 14 / 18 21 ↗ / 19 18 16 ↗ / 18
dar - lin', oh my dar - lin', oh my dar - lin' Clem - en - tine, You are
A7 D A7 D A7 D
19 / 18 16 18 14 / 18 16 ↗ 9 13 16 14 ↗
lost and gone for - ev - er, dread - ful sor - ry, Clem - en - tine.

2. Light she was, and like a fairy, and her shoes were number nine,
Herring boxes without topses, sandals were for Clementine. *(Chorus)*

3. Drove she ducklings to the water every morning just at nine,
Hit her foot against a splinter, fell into the foaming brine. *(Chorus)*

4. Ruby lips above the water, blowing bubbles soft and fine,
Sad for me! I was no swimmer, so I lost my Clementine. *(Chorus)*

By now you've discovered that the same melody string can be found in more than one chord. That's why you must be sure that the string you're plucking is located in the correct chord—the one that is harmonically suited to the melody being played. Study each song before you play it. Find out where the chords are and where the melody strings are located within that chord.

Remember, just aim for the area in which the numbered string is located. Several strings are blanked out on either side of that string, so you can't make a mistake if you have the correct chord. Now try the next song, using the same thumb brush (↑) where indicated, to keep the rhythm going.

JACOB'S LADDER

Chords Used: C, F, G7, G, & C7   Spiritual

    2. Rise, shine give God glory, (3)   4. Sinner, do you love your Jesus? (3)
        Soldiers of the Cross.   Soldiers of the Cross.

    3. Every rung goes higher, higher, (3)   5. If you love Him, why not serve Him, (3)
        Soldiers of the Cross.   Soldiers of the Cross.

After you've played "Jacob's Ladder" once, try playing the second verse an octave higher, starting on E, the 28th string. Of course, this is too high for many singers, but it makes a nice solo. If you have two Autoharpists you can play it as a duet.

This next arrangement of an old spiritual uses the Am chord to add depth and color, and the C, rather than the usual C7, for the running melody. You can play it either way. The first, as you'll see, has more of a folk quality. Although it's arranged in the lower octaves, as was the previous song, you can play it an octave higher as a solo melody piece.

NOBODY KNOWS THE TROUBLE I'VE SEEN

Chords Used: C, F, G, & Am

With feeling

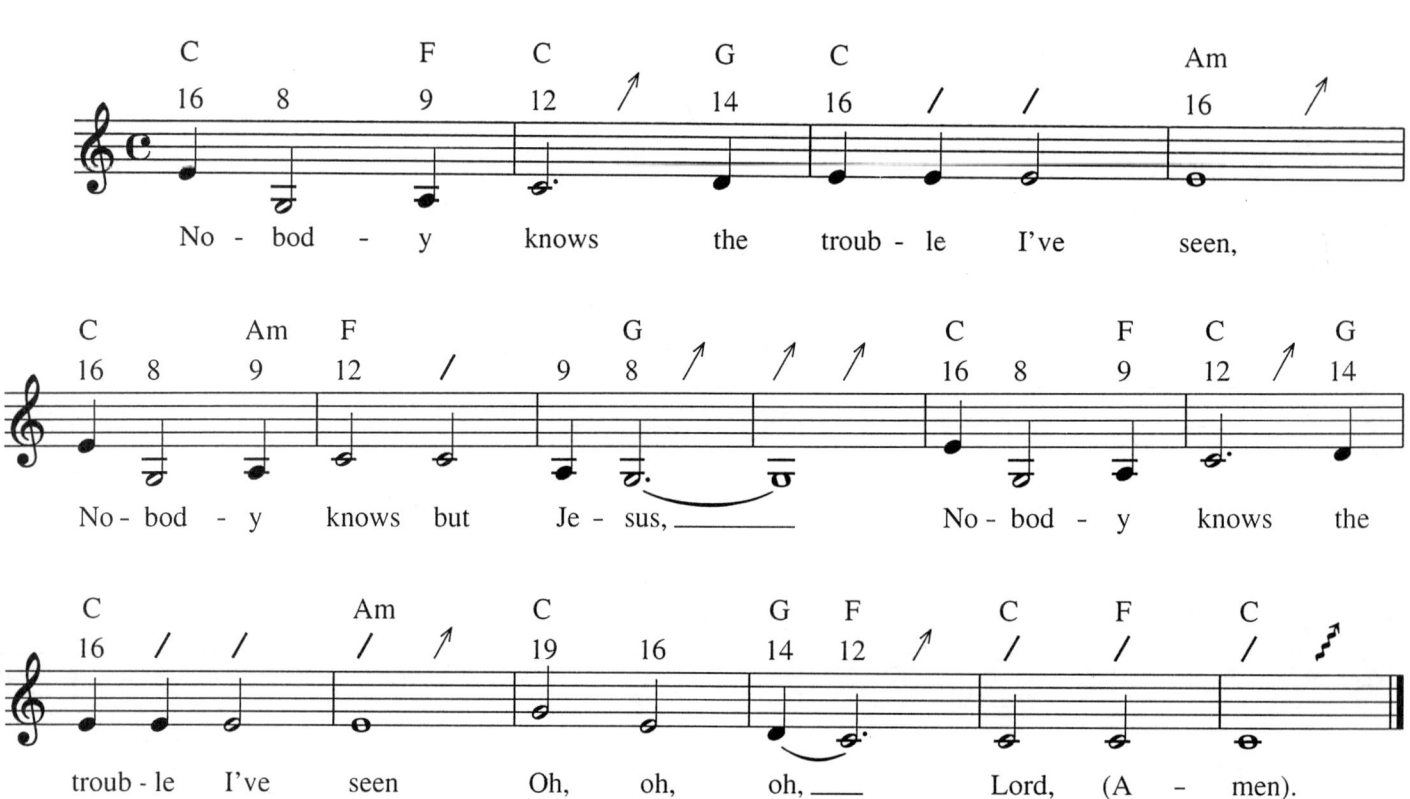

These next two pieces use straight melody picking with occasional thumb brushes () to keep the rhythm going. They're both chorded in the higher octaves, since that's the traditional Autoharp sound when it's played as a solo melody instrument. Naturally, if you're accompanying singing, you'd move to a lower key.

You've already played "Camptown Races," using the Thumb Lick in the key of D (p.43). Now try this melody arrangement in the key of F. Notice how the added F7 chord is used not only for color, but as a transition to the next phrase.

CAMPTOWN RACES

Chords Used: F, B♭, C7, & E7

Stephen Foster

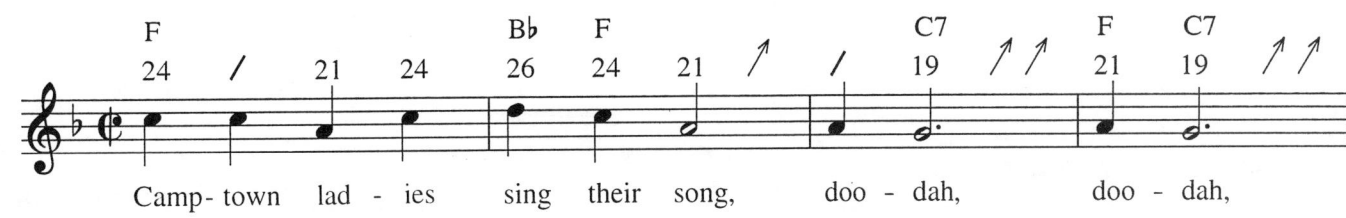

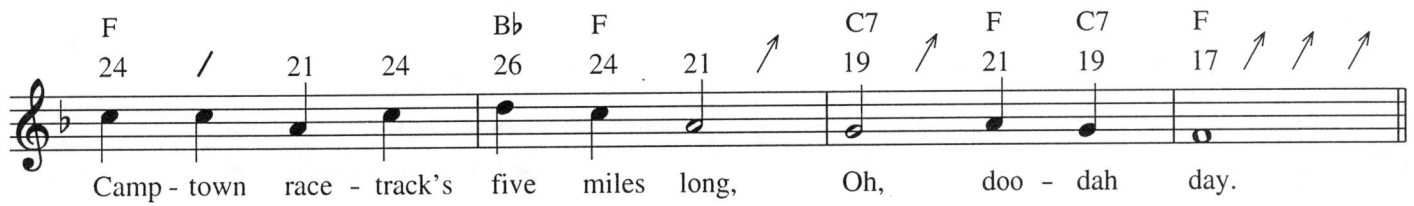

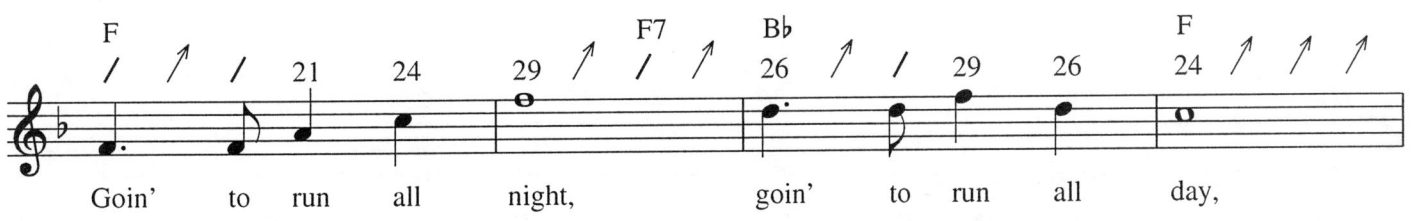

The added number of chord change makes this next song a real challenge!

BATTLE HYMN OF THE REPUBLIC

Chords Used: C, F, G7, E7, C7, Am, & Dm

FILLER STROKES
Thumb – brush

You've already used a simple filler stroke—a rhythmic upstroke with the thumb to fill in the "spaces" between melody notes. Now you'll use a gentle up-down brush with the thumb, which you learned earlier in Strum #5, p.30. As I pointed out, this is the foundation of all country and mountain strumming, and must be done delicately, without scratching, using a rotating wrist.

Start practicing this up-down combination (↑↓) slowly, in the lower octave, then speed it up. It should hardly sound, giving the song momentum, but not overpowering the melody. So you won't be confused about the number of fillers per measure, count the second measure of the next song like this:

1	&	2	&	3	&	4	&
Pinch	up – down	up – down	up – down	up – down	Pinch	Pinch	Pinch

Of course, each measure is slightly different, but by counting out loud in this manner, you will soon feel the correct rhythm. Notice how the thumb automatically opens up for the pinch after the last series of fillers.

LONESOME VALLEY

Chords Used: F, B♭, C7, & F7

Slow tempo

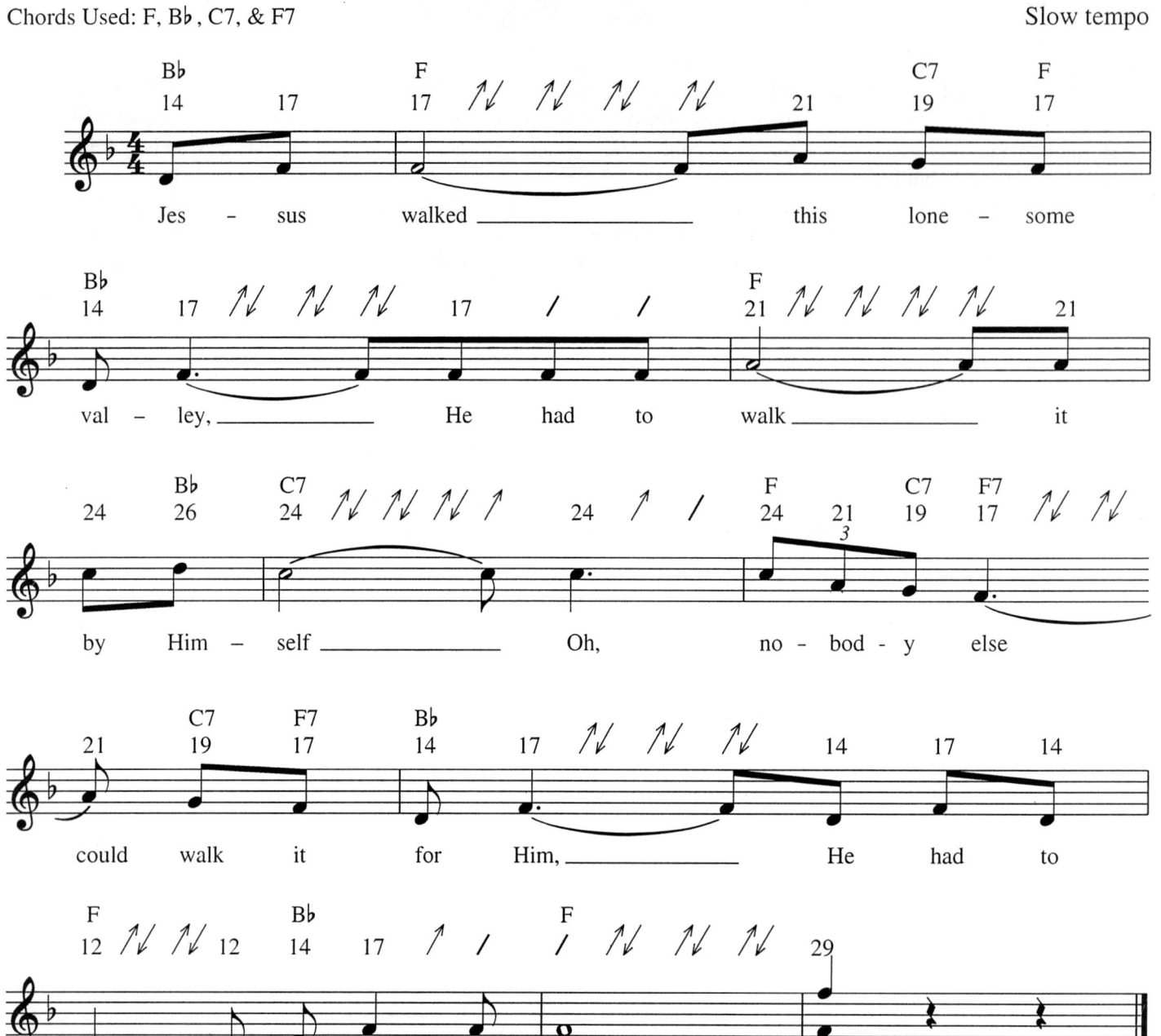

2. You must go and stand your trial;
   You have to stand it by yourself,
   Oh, nobody else can stand it for you;
   You'll have to stand it by yourself.

Another good way to practice the thumb brushes is to press down any chord, then start slowly, saying out loud as you play: **Pinch, up-down, up-down, up-down** several times. Next move to **Pinch, up-down, up-down,** and finally, speed up the tempo to play **Pinch, up-down, Pinch, up-down.** Again you'll notice how the thumb opens up automatically, after the fast up-down strokes, in preparation for the next pinch. Be sure not to wiggle the thumb, but keep it straight during the stroke. And, of course, rotate the wrist smoothly.

First, practice:

Pinch, up-down, up-down, Pinch, up-down, up-down

Repeat this filler several times before applying it to the next folk song, which you've already played as a simple two-chord accompaniment in the key of C (p.14). Now change to the key of G and see how much more interesting the tune sounds in melody picking style.

Remember that every time you see a slash (/) it means to pinch—to repeat the previous melody string and chord. If there is a new chord, but the melody string remains the same, it will appear above the slash.

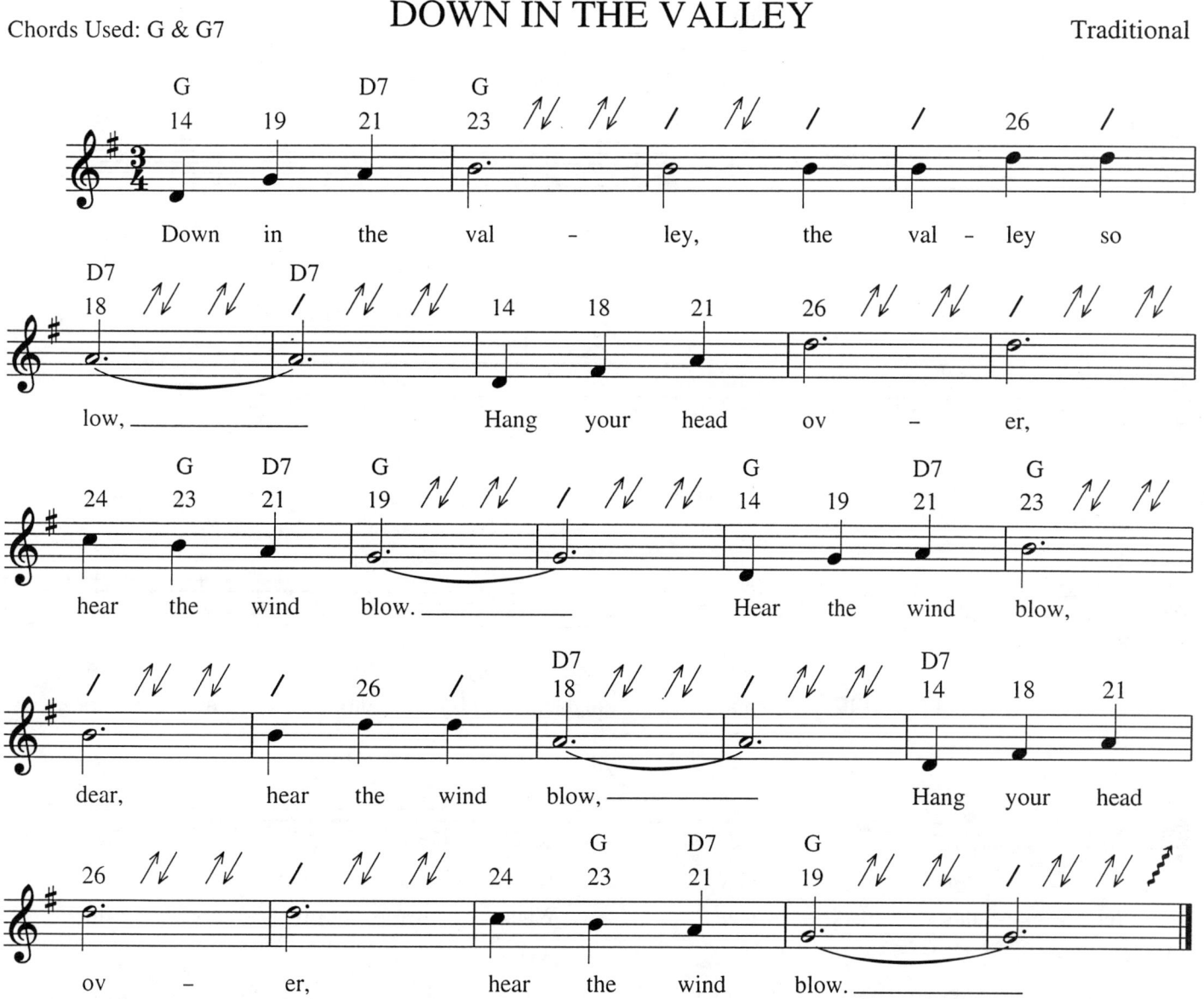

2. Roses love sunshine, violets love dew;
   Angels in heaven know I love you.
   Know I love you, dear, know I love you.
   Angels in heaven know I love you.

3. Build me a castle forty miles high,
   So I can see him as he rides by;
   As he rides by, dear, as he rides by;
   So I can see him as he rides by.

This next melody is a lot harder, because of the speed of the filler strokes. They must be done very delicately, or the picks will catch on the strings and make an unpleasant scratching sound.

"Wildwood Flower" was one of the late Mother Maybelle Carter's favorites and is excellent for practicing the **Pinch, up-down, Pinch, up-down** sequence. Notice how the Pinch is used as an integral part of the filler, rather than just repeating the up-down thumb strokes over and over. You can also use small pinches up and down the strings during the long spaces in the melody. Experiment with fillers and you'll find many ways to add variety to your playing while keeping the rhythm of the piece going.

FILLER STROKES

Thumb-index

Many Autoharp pickers, especially those who also play guitar, use alternating thumb (T = ↗) and index finger (i = ↙) strokes for fillers, rather than just stroking with the thumb alone. This is a good introduction to advanced mountain picking, where, eventually, the thumb will strike the melody string and the index finger will play the rhythmic filler on the second half of the beat.*

This old folk song will help you perfect these delicate, fast filler strokes. You can play a pinch on the melody notes and a T i (Thumb-index) filler in between, or you can play the melody with an accented thumb upstroke and, as indicated over the first line of music, a T i up-down stroke when needed to keep the beat going.

Practice the alternating thumb-index strokes with a rotating wrist, going up and down with the music, until you "hear" the melody emerge.

GO TELL AUNT RHODY

Chords Used: G & D7   Lively

2. The one she's been saving (three times)
   To make a feather bed.

3. She died in the mill pond (three times)
   A standin' on her head.

4. The goslins are mournin' (three times)
   Because their mother's dead,

You'll find that slower songs like "Oh, Bury Me Not On the Lone Prairie" and "I've Got Peace Like a River," (p.38) are well suited for this kind of thumb-index filler. Since it would be awkward to pinch after the index downstroke, the melody note following the filler is almost always played with a thumb upstroke.

---

*For extensive study in filler strokes and the single string thumb tap as used in country and bluegrass picking: *Mel Bay's Complete Book of Traditional and Country Autoharp Picking Styles* by Meg Peterson, Mel Bay Publications, 1986, Pacific, MO 63069.

SUMMARY OF MELODY PICKING

1. The Autoharp strings are numbered from 1 (low F) to 36 (high C). Each number indicates the location of the melody string.

2. The proper chord in which that string is located is placed above the number. Chords will be written once and not repeated between chord changes.

3. A slash / means to repeat the previous melody string (note) and chord, unless a new chord is indicated.

4. An arrow ↗ is a gentle upstroke with the thumb in the lower octave to keep the beat going.

5. Pinch whenever you see a number or a slash.

Those of you who are proficient in melody picking, or who can hear the melody as you play, will not need the numbers or the melody aid. For this reason the chord designations have been placed above the numbers so your eye can easily follow the changes. Numbers, however, will still be helpful if you are unfamiliar with the tune and wish to check the location of a particular melody string.

Once you have learned to use the chart on p.63, fig. 29, you can make your own melody arrangements. First, determine the chord in which the melody note is located, then use the chart to find the string numbers. Start with the songs already learned earlier in this book, and simply add more chord changes as the melody requires. This is usually the 7th chord of the key in which you are playing. Hundreds of songs can be played this way on the Autoharp. Experiment, try new and more difficult harmonies, and above all **practice** until the chord combinations automatically fall into place under your fingers.

RHYTHM PICKING

There are an infinite number of rhythms that can be played on the Autoharp, building on the twenty basic strum patterns presented in this book. Rhythm picking is more concerned with playing these various rhythms than with playing melody. Therefore, in the following arrangements there will be fewer chord changes and no more string numbers under the chord designations.

The techniques set forth draw heavily on guitar and banjo picking, without the need to hit exact strings—only approximate areas of each octave. The octaves chosen for a particular strum depend on the style most comfortable for the player. The combinations of strokes are numerous within each rhythmic category.

These more advanced strums can be played using the thumb, index, and middle finger, or a flat pick as in fig. 31. The Autoharp is best held Appalachian style for freer arm and finger movement.

Figure 31
Playing Appalachian Style with a Flat Pick

CALYPSO

Calypso music, popularly identified with Trinidad, has its roots in the polyrhythms of both Spain and Africa. It has become the musical trademark of the British West Indies and along with reggae, an offshoot from Jamaica, has greatly influenced the rock scene around the world.

Syncopation is the rhythmic characteristic of calypso. This means that the two main stresses (accents) in each measure are divided unequally instead of equally as in most American folk songs. Think of syncopation as a "misplaced" accent.

A typical calypso rhythm divides each bar into eight parts, with accents on the first and fourth parts. This feeling can be adapted to the Autoharp by using a combination of up and down strokes played with the index finger alone, the thumb and index finger alternating, or a flat pick. No octave designations are noted, because the pattern can be played in any octave. Before playing, clap the rhythm, accenting the beat where indicated. After you have the feeling in your hands, apply the strum to the Autoharp.

Count:	**1**	&	2	**&**	3	&	4	&
	↑	↓	↑	↓	↑	↓	↑	↓
	up >	down	up	**down** >	up	down	up	down

Clap and play the pattern several time. Repeat the direction of the strokes out loud, being sure to accent the first and fourth. Always use a rotating wrist motion.

Once you have played this rhythm several times, **leave out the fifth stroke like this:**

Strum #21

Count:	1	&	2	&	3	&	4	&
	↑	↓	↑	↓	❼ *	↓	↑	↓
	up >	down	up	**down** >	(pause)	down	up	down

* = an 8th note rest. This represents a pause in the strum. Do not play when you see this symbol.

In order to master this strum, think of the wrist as rotating constantly, even when there is a pause (rest) in the pattern. Keep thinking:

one - and	two - and	(rest) - and	four - and
up - down	up - down	(pause) - down	up - down

Say and play this over and over again until you have the rhythm in your fingers. Even though you won't sound the strings when there's a pause, the arm motion will continue, so your hand will be in the correct position for the next downstoke.

As in previous strums, the pattern will only be printed above the first line of music, but should be played throughout the song. Remember, the slash marks / / / indicate the basic beat of the piece.

THE SLOOP "JOHN B"

Chords Used: G, C, D7, G7, & Am

Calypso

Play the tune, again, in the middle octave. Notice how the melody is brought out just by changing chords more frequently, especially from the I (G) to the V7 (D7) in the key of G.

This next piece is typical of so many calypso songs—repetative and not afraid to deal with everyday life, no matter how mundane. As you sing it you'll also find that, in an attempt to fit the lyrics into the rhythm, the emphasis is often placed on a syllable not normally stressed. This is a challenge to many North American folk singers.

Try a variation on Strum #21, using the middle finger to play the downstroke after the rest. It will automatically reach for the higher octave and give the song a different, brighter sound. The thumb and index finger will play in the middle octave.

Strum #21a

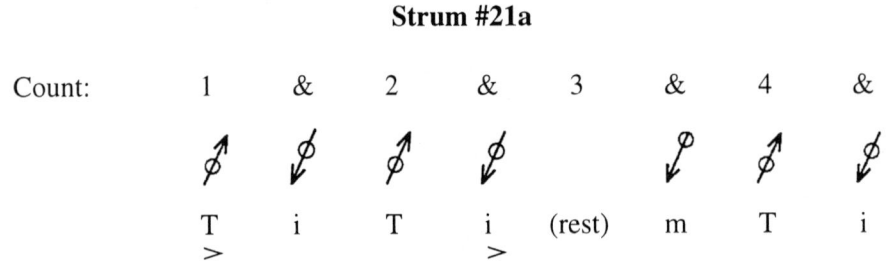

EVERYBODY LOVES SATURDAY NIGHT

Chords Used: F & C7

Brightly

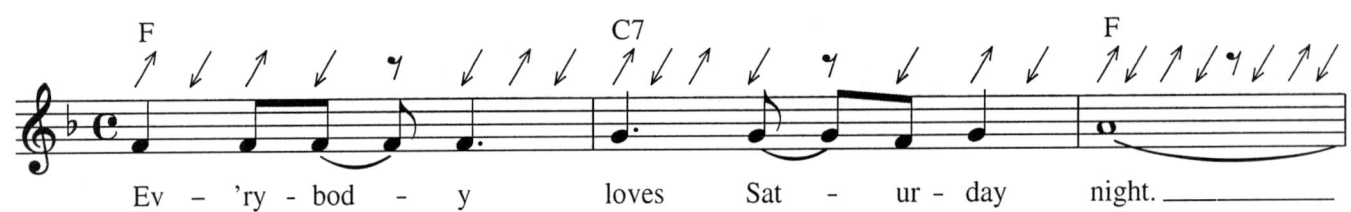

(Continue Strum)

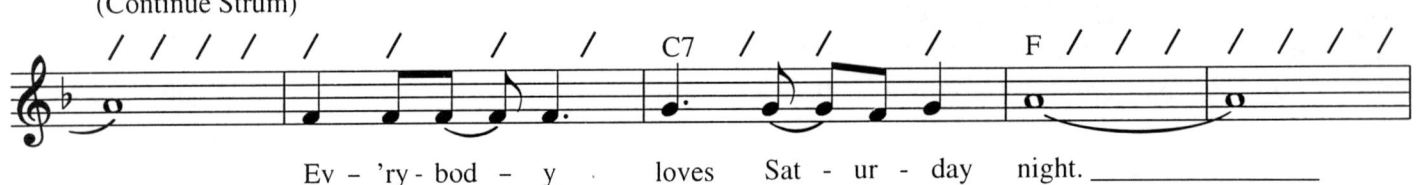

When you play calypso rhythms you can use many other strokes and combinations of strokes, including the arpeggiando, sequential pinches, the rasqueado, the rasqueado backwards, and Travis strums.* The most important thing is to keep the syncopation going, even when the verse is sung in a slightly different rhythm.

* For further study of Calypso strums: *The Complete Method for Autoharp® or Chormaharp*, by Meg Peterson, 1979, pp., 83-89

BLUES AND JAZZ

Blues and jazz are both musical expressions of the Black experience in America. The blues came first, long before it emerged commercially in the 1900s, and developed from Black work songs and spirituals. As with jazz, it dealt with basic feelings—the troubles, pain, joy, humor, and struggle of everyday life in the deep South.

There are two basic rhythms—triplet and shuffle—that you will use to play both blues and jazz tunes.

TRIPLET RHYTHM

In the triplet form you play three evenly spaced strokes on each beat. You can use a flat pick as in figure 31, p.77, or your index finger, striking the strings with the nail. There are no octave designations on the next pattern, for it is a driving rhythm that can be played in either the lower or higher octaves, depending on the intensity of the song.

Strum #22

```
         ⌒ 3 ⌒      ⌒ 3 ⌒      ⌒ 3 ⌒      ⌒ 3 ⌒
Count::  1  &  uh   2  &  uh   3  &  uh   4  &  uh
         ↑  ↑  ↑    ↑  ↑  ↑    ↑  ↑  ↑    ↑  ↑  ↑
         i  i  i    i  i  i    i  i  i    i  i  i
```

As you practice, count out loud: 1 da da, 2 da da, or 1 and uh, 2 and uh, etc., keeping the strokes short, even and adding a slight forward momentum as the piece reaches its climax.

You've already played the next tune using a simple strum in the key of C. Now play it in the key of G with added 7th chords to give it a country blues sound. Notice how it ends on a 7th chord, an harmonic structure found predominantly in blues melodies.

CARELESS LOVE

Chords Used: G, C, D7, G7, A7, & C7

Traditional folk

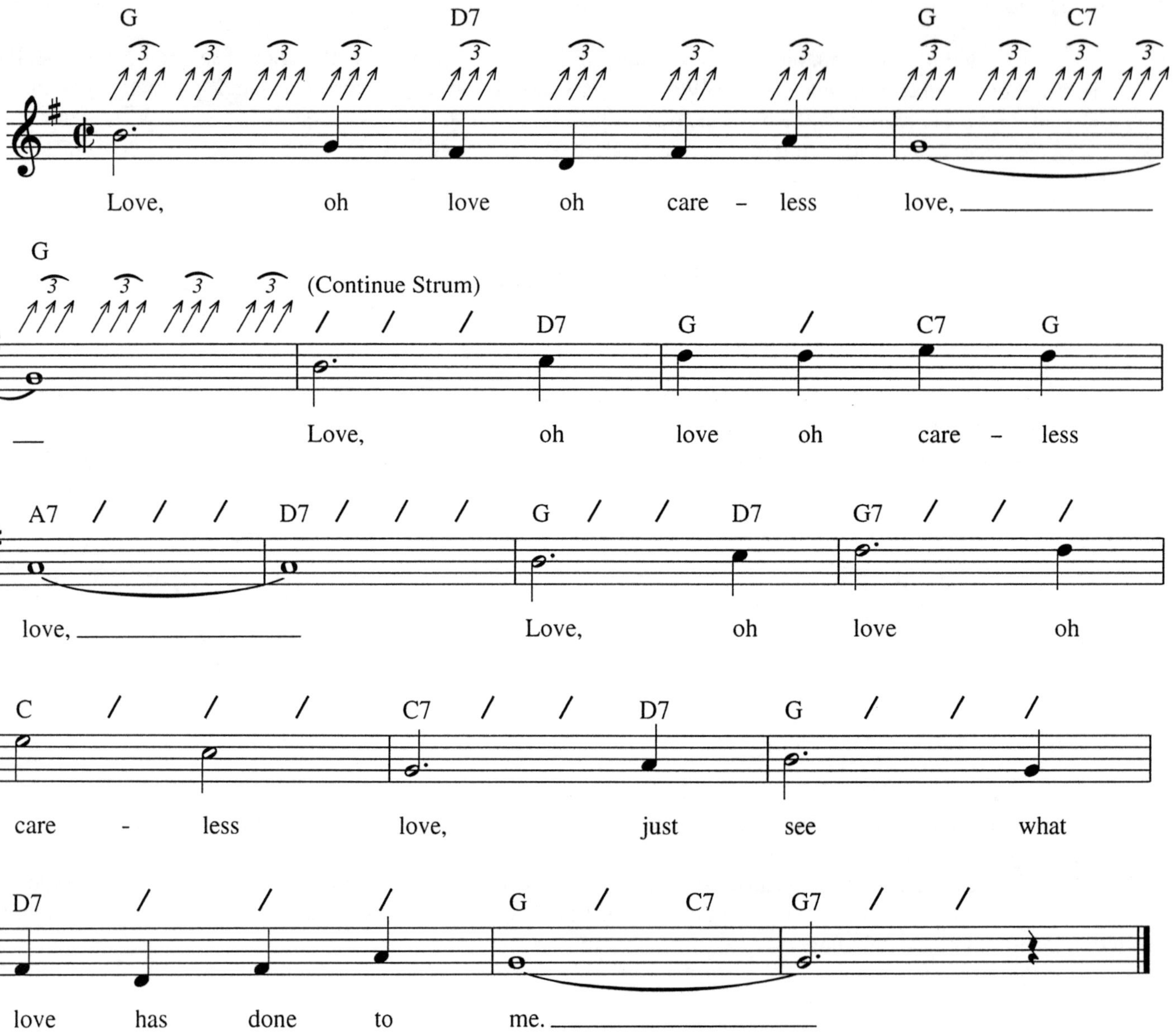

Love, oh love oh care - less love, _____
Love, oh love oh care - less
love, _____ Love, oh love oh
care - less love, just see what
love has done to me. _____

Now change the fingering slightly, using the thumb on the upstrokes and the index finger on the downstrokes like this:

Strum #22a

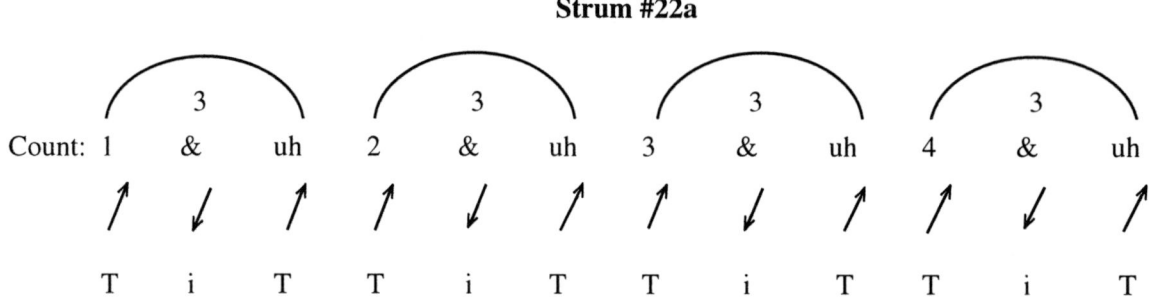

Although the next piece is an old folk song, it can be given a blues feeling by using the triplet rhythm. You may notice that it has a very common chord sequence—repeated throughout the song—that is used in many modern rock songs: F, Dm, Gm, and C7. You may want to use picks on your thumb and index finger for added clarity.

I LOVE THE MOUNTAINS

Chords Used: F, Dm, Gm, & C7
Traditional folk

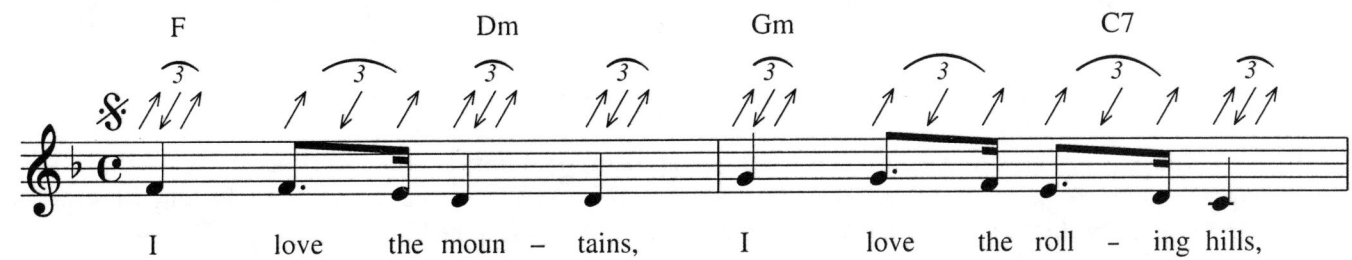

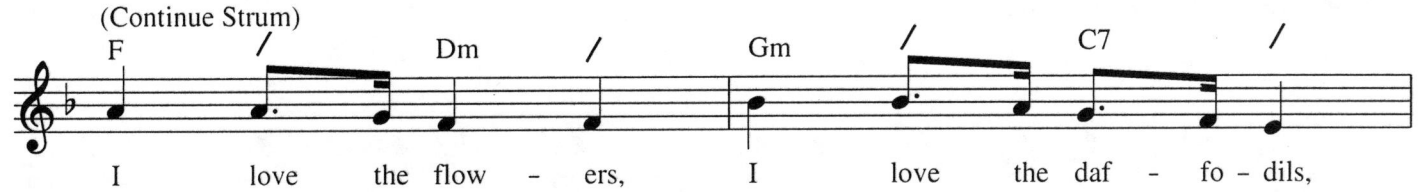

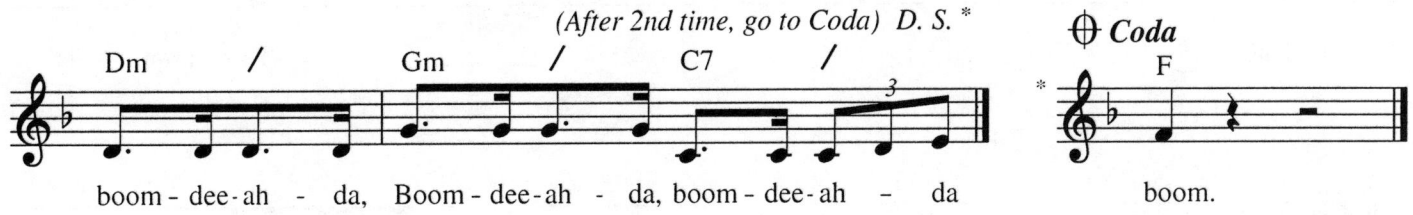

* D. S. = An abbreviation for Dal Segno, which means "from the sign" (𝄋).
Coda = An ending section of a musical piece, symbolized as ⊕.

SHUFFLE RHYTHM

Shuffle rhythm is counted the same as triplet rhythm, but the middle stroke (the "&") is left out and the "uh" stroke is lightly accented. It is played in the middle octave with the thumb and index fingers, a flat pick, or a loose fist as seen in figures 19 and 20, p.39. Rather than a smooth, straight rhythm, there is a slight hesitation at the end of each beat, which gives it the improvisatory sound of the blues.

Strum #23

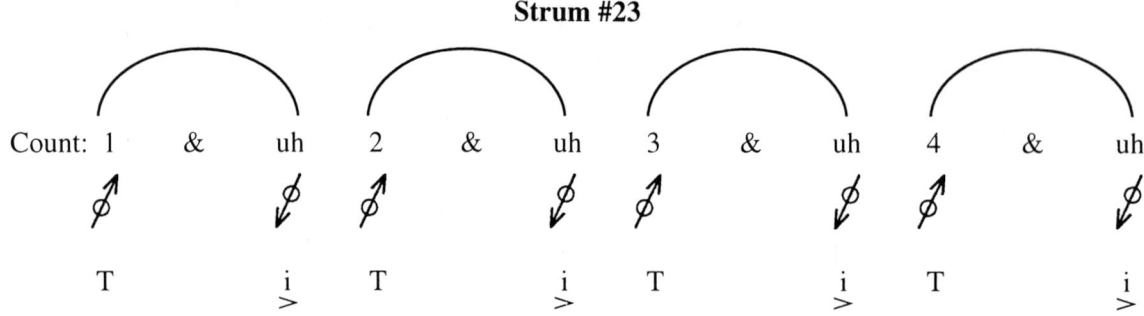

As you practice this strum, count out loud "dum - de - dum - de - dum - de - dum - de," accenting the shorter down stroke rather than the initial upstroke. There is almost a syncopated feel to the beat as you sing the song while playing a slightly different rhythm. You will soon discover that you have to **feel** the blues.

THIS TRAIN

Chords Used: D, G, A7, D7, & G7   Traditional

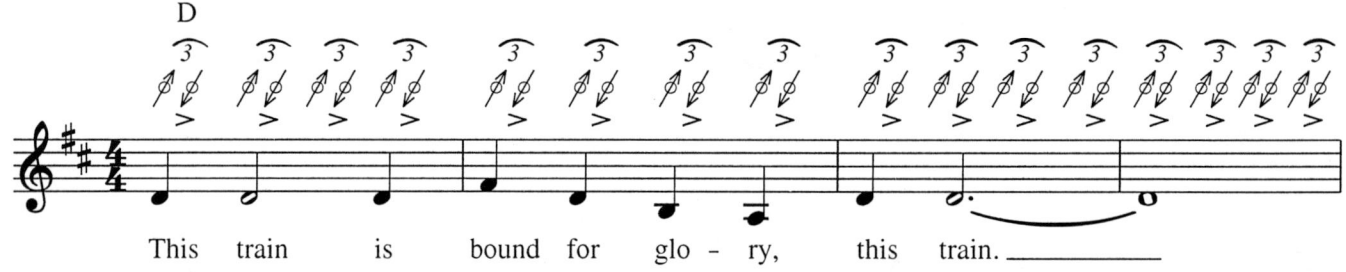

This train don't carry no gamblers, this train
This train don't carry no gamblers, this train
This train don't carry no gamblers,
No crap shooters, no midnight ramblers,
This train is bound for glory, this train.

Now try combining the shuffle and the triplet rhythms, by playing a straight shuffle strum for three beats and adding a triplet figure on the final beat.

Strum #23a

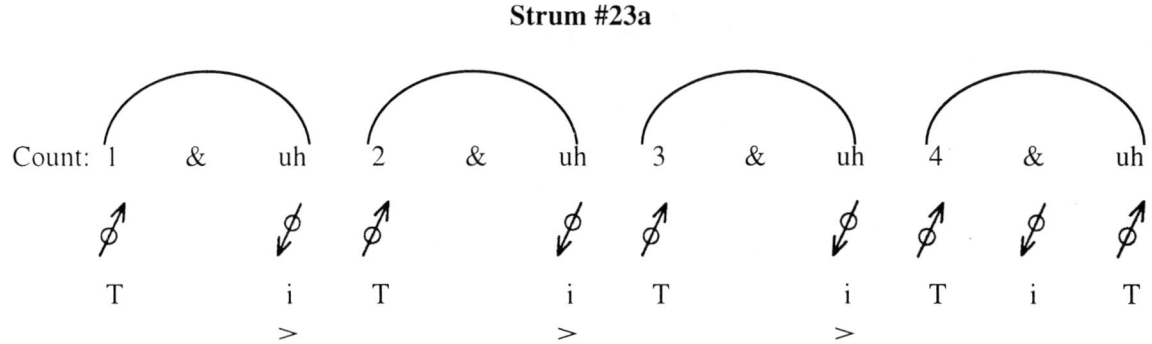

See how you can take this old folk song, which you've already played in the key of C (p.33), and give it a completely different sound by using a blues strum.

HE'S GOT THE WHOLE WORLD IN HIS HANDS

Chords Used: D, A7, G7, & D7   Traditional

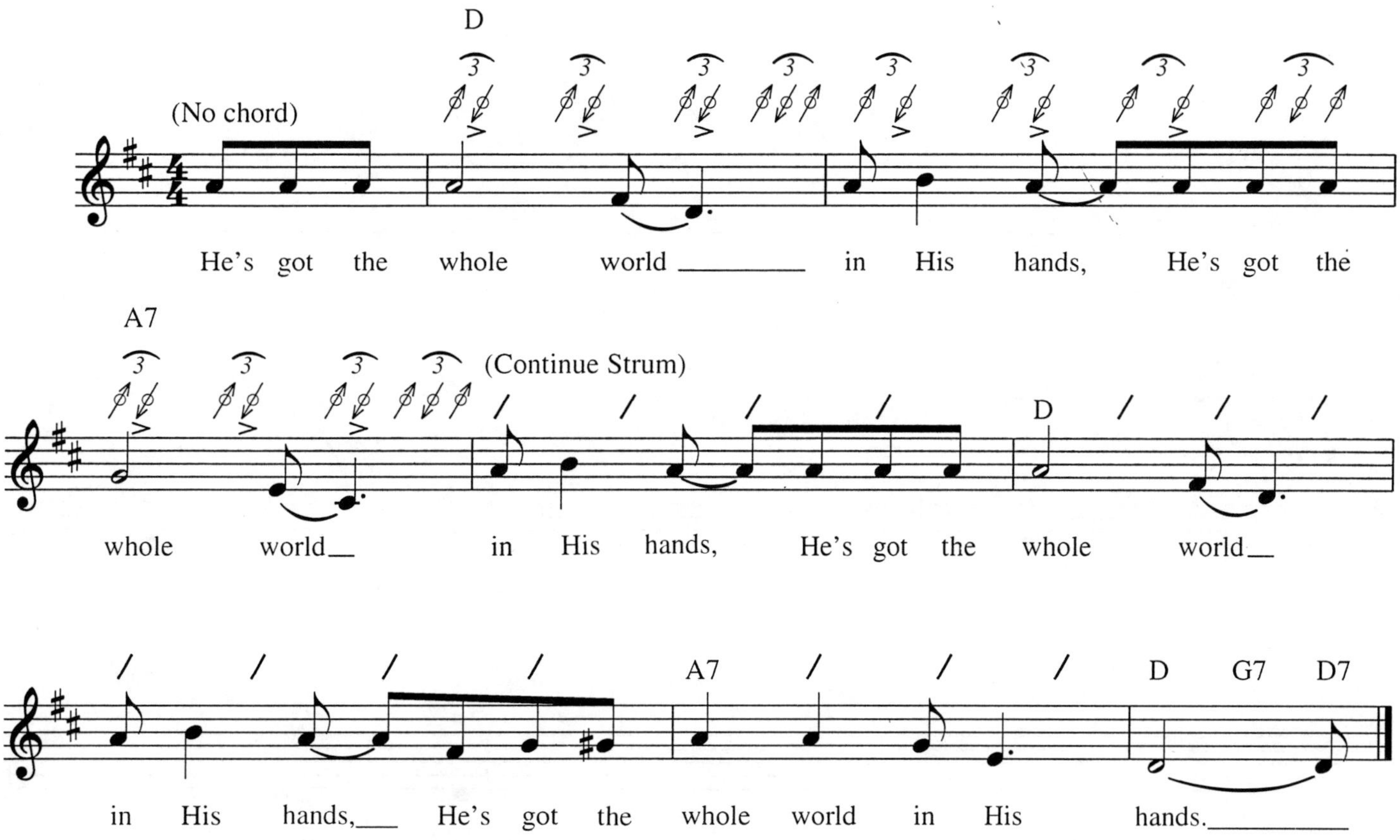

Now try playing the same song, using the loose fist or a flat pick, instead of the thumb and index finger. You'll soon discover for yourself the combination of strokes and fingers that lend a unique sound to your playing.

DOUBLE THUMBING

Using the basic shuffle rhythm, move the thumb from the lower to the middle octave on the count of 2 and 4. The index finger stays in the same area, playing short downstrokes, while the thumb alternates with upstrokes, first in the lower, then in the middle octave.

Strum #24

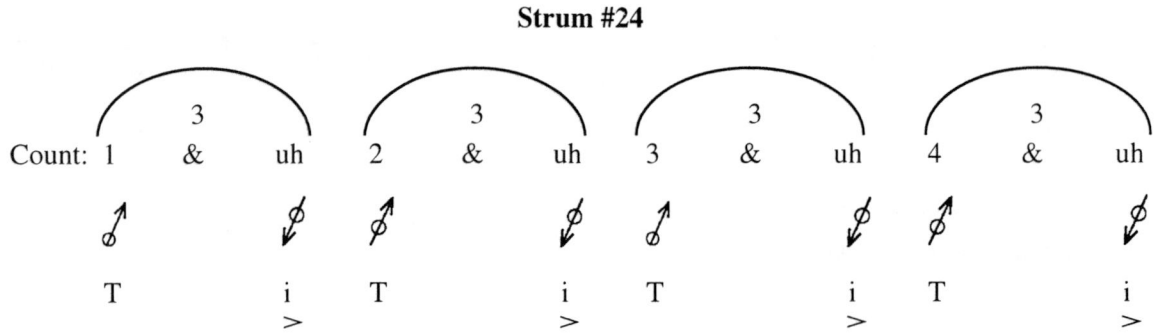

JOE TURNER

Chords Used: C, F7, & G7   Traditional blues

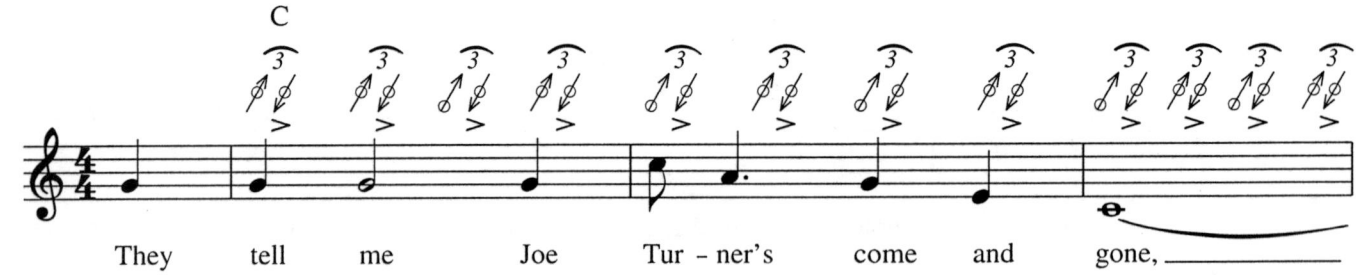

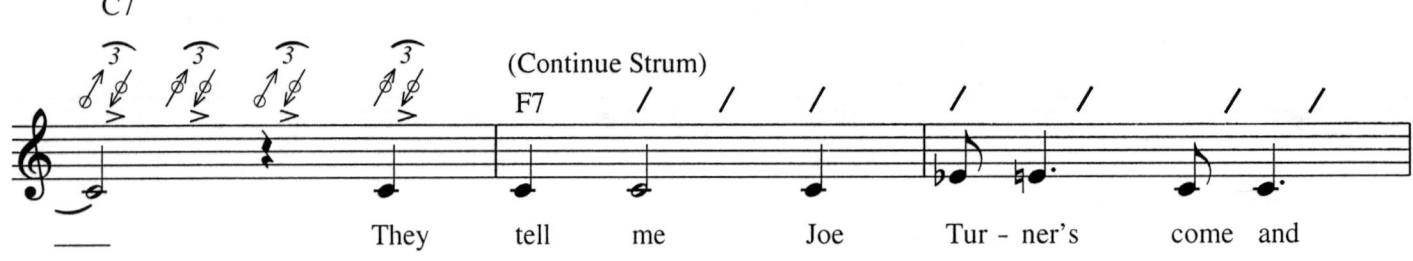

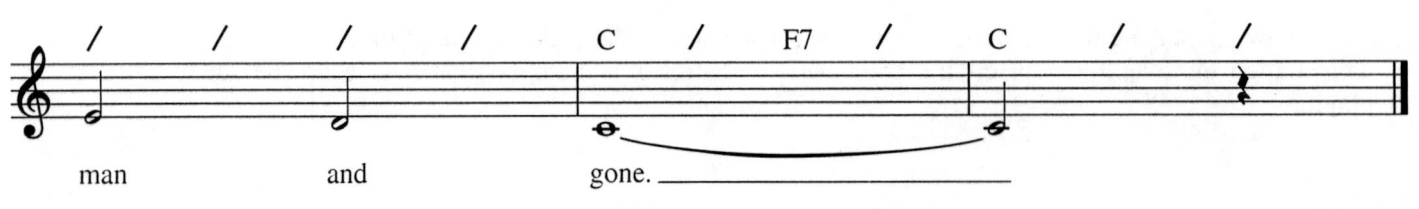

THE ROCKER STRUM

The rocker strum, widely used in early jazz and blues, is very similar to double thumbing, except that the thumb and index finger move up and down the three octaves of the Autoharp like a boogie woogie walking bass. The strum is more interesting if you play each short stroke in a different section of the specified octave. As with double thumbing, the shuffle rhythm is maintained throughout the pattern.

This next strum is played twice in each measure, because of the slow tempo of the song.

Strum #25

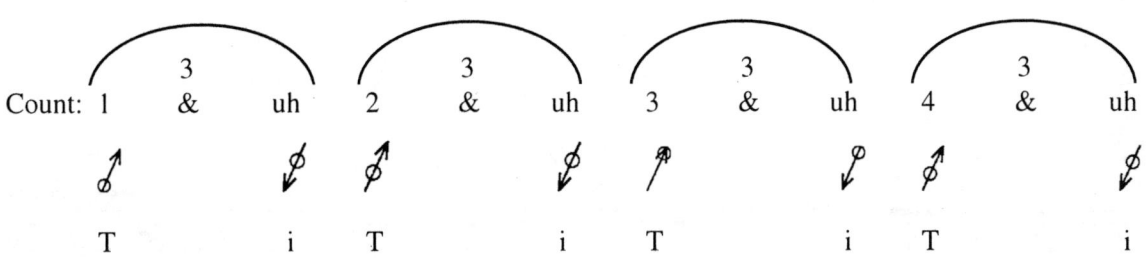

This next song came out of the early jazz movement in New Orleans called Dixieland—not the sophisticated music we know today. It was used at a typical Black funeral procession in the Old South, played mournfully on the way to the cemetery. On the return from the graveside, another song already learned in this book, "When the Saints Go Marching In," (p.40) was played joyfully, with trumpets and clarinets accompanied by much singing and dancing.

JUST A CLOSER WALK WITH THEE

Chords Used: G, C, D7 & G7

Slowly

For variety, try adding syncopation to the shuffle rhythm by resting on the first part of the third beat. This is similar to a calypso strum with a shuffle beat and can be used not only on early jazz and blues tunes, but also many old spirituals and gospel songs that had their origin in the Black experience.

To take advantage of the upper strings, play the second half of the third beat with an accented downstroke with the middle finger in the higher octave.

Strum #26

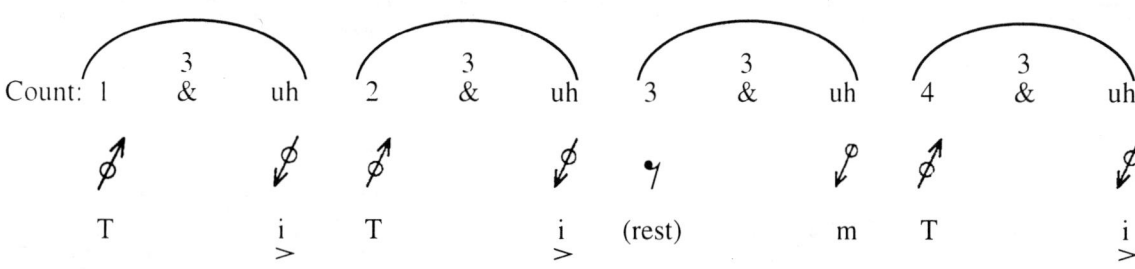

THIS LITTLE LIGHT OF MINE

Chords Used: G, C, D7, G7, C7, (B7), & (Em)

Brightly

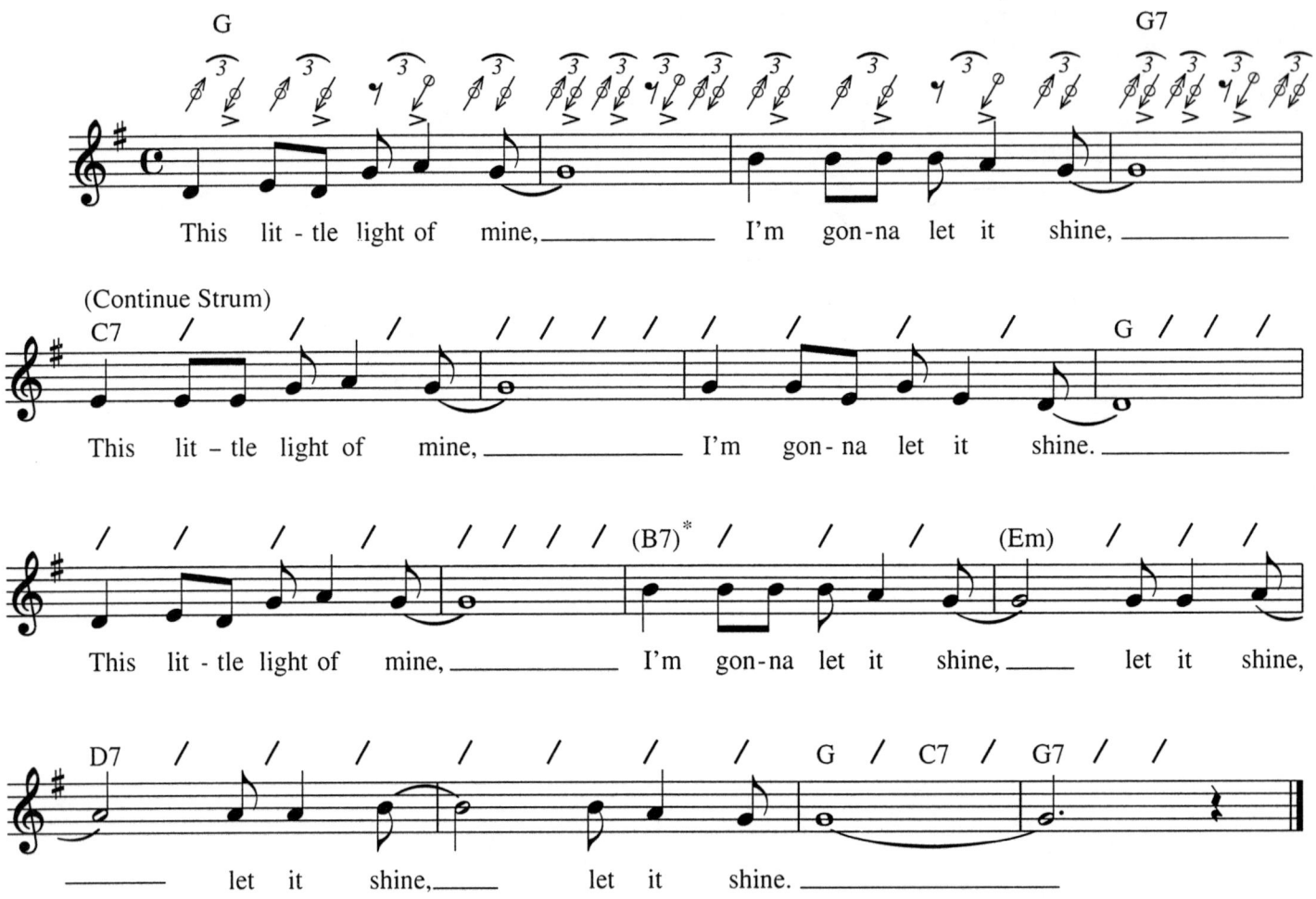

*Chords in parentheses are optional. These are only available on the 21 chord Autoharp. If you don't want to use them, stay on the previous chord. You will be harmonically correct.

> The key to jazz and blues is improvisation in words and music. You can create your own blues songs, using a typical 12 or 16 bar chord progression.* Pick a blues progression and play it over and over again. Next, make up an original melody to fit the chord sequence. Do the same with the words, repeating the first two lines, and changing the words and the tune on the last line. Sing about everyday subjects, some sad, some joyous. Use combinations of the triplet and shuffle rhythm, and experiment with syncopated and arpeggio patterns that you've learned earlier in this book. Use the thumb, index finger, middle finger, a loose fist, or a flat pick. Be sure to put real emotion into your song and make the Autoharp speak for you.
>
> *For further study of blues progressions and composing your own songs, see p. 104, *The Complete Method for Autoharp® or Chromaharp* by Meg Peterson, Mel Bay Publication, Pacific, MO 63069, 1979.

Use a typical folk-rock strum on this last tune, playing the shuffle rhythm of strum #23 (p. 84) with a loose fist on the upstroke and an accented brush with the fingernail of the thumb on the downstroke. This requires a firm, clock-like precision as you rotate the wrist. The pattern is written like this:

Strum #27

ROCK – A – MY – SOUL

Chords Used: F & C7
Traditional

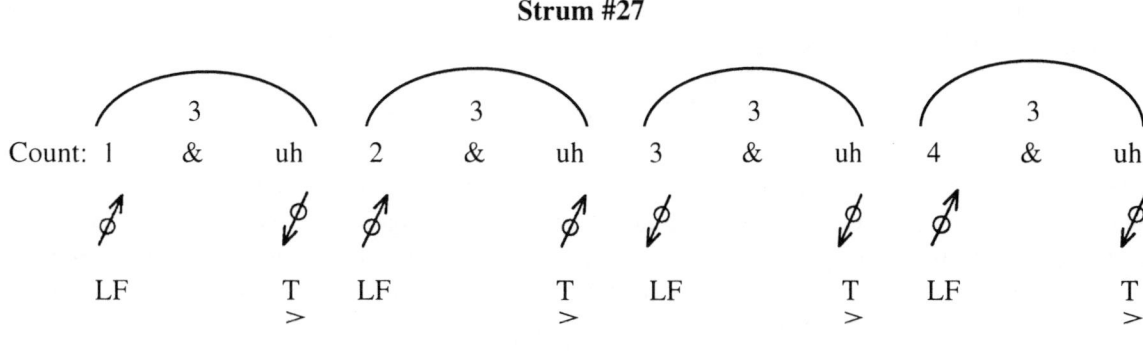

2. So high, you can't get over it (3 times)
   Oh, rock – a – my soul.

3. So low you can't get under it... (3 times)

4. So wide you can't get 'round of it... (3 times)

5. Rock – a – my soul in the bosom of Abraham... (3 times)

The influence and endurance of the early blues and jazz rhythms are evident to anyone who listens to the jazz, country, and rock hits of today.

You can use these last eight strum patterns on many rock and folk-rock songs. Don't hesitate to combine the triplet and shuffle rhythm in the same song, adding variety and excitement to the song. The triplet rhythm can be very emotional when used with a crescendo and a steady driving beat. And the shuffle rhythm can be played in many different ways in the various octaves, fast or slow, to denote a variety of feelings. But always use imagination and an improvisational style rather than a rigid, meticulous approach.

IN CONCLUSION...

There are many other kinds of music—ragtime, flamenco, rhythm and blues, rock, reggae, and Dixieland—that can be played on the Autoharp. Time and space do not allow a full examination of all of them in this book. I suggest, however, that you experiment with your favorite type of music and incorporate your understanding of melody picking with the thirty-three strums you've just learned, to invent and perfect your own special style. And, most importantly, I urge you to continue to grow and expand your repertoire of Autoharp music and technique by attending folk festivals and workshops, and joining a folk music club or a group of Autoharp enthusiasts in your area. If you have no club where you live, start one. If you want help in this endeavor and information about Autoharp activities around the country, get in touch with fellow Autoharpists through the *Autoharp Quarterly,* P.O. Box A, Newport, PA 17074.

If you have the opportunity, take a course in music at an adult school or college where you live. There are many and they can only broaden your appreciation of music, music theory, and the part that other instruments play in the richness of our musical heritage.

Share your music with others, whether as a soloist in a café or concert hall or as a volunteer at a hospital, nursing home, or other health care facility. Play for children, help out in school assembly programs, put on a musical program at your church or synagogue. Be a music maker, not just a listener.

Above all, keep playing and keep enjoying. Music is food for the soul, communication at its highest level. And participating actively in its pursuit is what lifts life out of the mundane into the magical. This is what I wish for you.

Keep strumming!

Meg Peterson

CASSETTE TAPE SPECIAL

INSTRUCTION CASSETTE to be used with this book. Meg Peterson takes you step by step through the major styles presented in *You Can Teach Yourself Autoharp.* Songs showing each style will be repeated, unaccompanied, giving you a chance to play along with the singer on your own. Attend a workshop right in your own living room!
Retail: $10.95; Postage: $2.50; Total: $13.45.

STAY IN TUNE WITH MEG PETERSON is a cassette tape showing two ways to tune the Autoharp. Additional tips on instrument care and string changing are included.
Retail: $9.95; Postage $2.50; Total: $12.45

Total retail value of both tapes: $25.90.

SPECIAL INTRODUCTORY PRICE FOR BOTH CASSETTES COMBINED:
$19.00 (including postage & handling)

Send check or money order in American dollars to:
Meg Peterson
33 South Pierson Rd.
Maplewood, NJ 07040

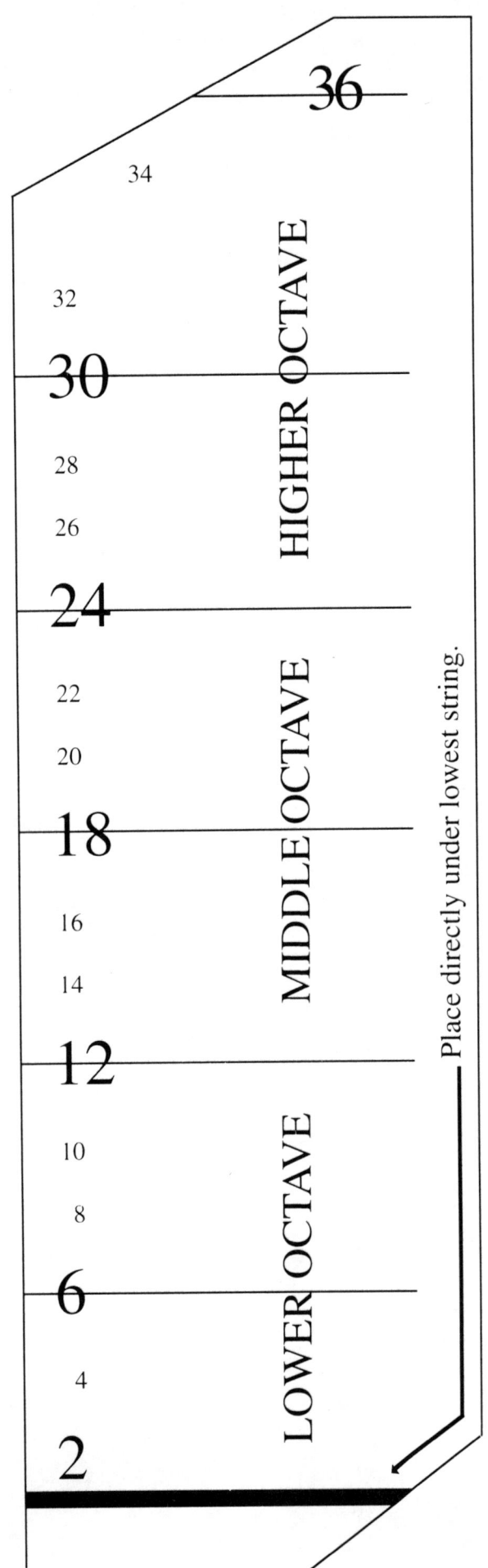
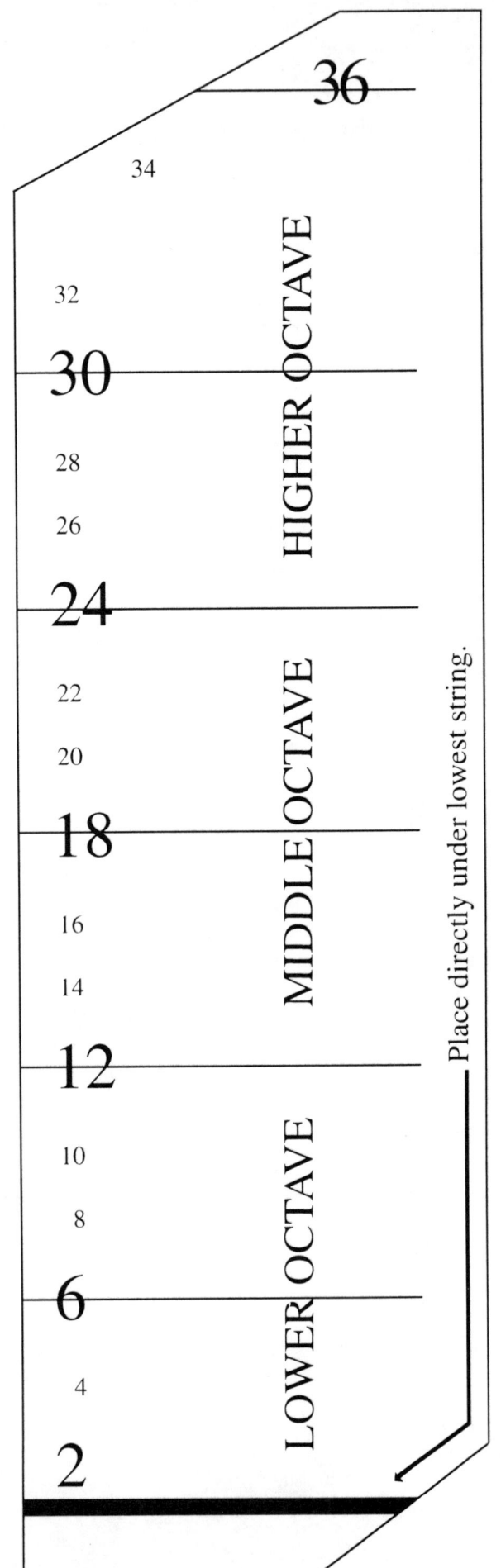